Stolen Hearts

Book One: More Than Treasure

Christy Newton

-ARC-

Lola,
Enjoy!
Christy Newton

ISBN-13: 978-1492738374
ISBN-10: 1492738379

Front Porch Romance
Division of D&D Publishig

DEDICATION

For my husband, without his love and support I would have never finished this book and my daughters who generously share mom with her characters. If I have to live in the real world, I'm happy it's with the three of you.
I love you all so much.

ACKNOWLEDGMENTS

I need to thank my mom for being my biggest fan, my brother for his support and the rest of my family for their encouragement. My critique partner, Danielle Doolittle – you made my writing shine. My beta reader, Crystal Holloway. My Scribbler Sisters: Danielle, Monica, Sue, Nancy and Misty – you all keep me going! My Publisher, Madison Connors who gave me my first yes.

Thank you and I love you all!

Chapter One

Cammie strolled out of the bathroom wrapped in a thick towel. Like every morning, her eyes were drawn to the space above her bed. Only this time when she glanced over to the wall, instead of smiling, a shrill scream escaped her lips. Grabbing her cell phone off the side table, she dialed with shaky fingers.

"911, what is your emergency?"

"This is Cammie Adams at 415 Brandy Way," she whispered, terrified. "I've been robbed and I'm not sure if they're still here." She peeked into the dark, empty hallway. Her body, paralyzed by fear, was unwilling to go any further.

"Stay on the line with me. I'm dispatching someone now."

Cammie's heart pounded in her ears. "Okay." She walked over to her purse on the chair and removed her stun gun. Remembering she was in a towel, she snatched a sundress out of her closet and slipped it over her head. The light fabric stuck to her damp skin. *What if the thief is inside the house?*

"Ma'am, are you still there?" The sound of the operator's voice made her jump.

"Yes." She closed her eyes and tried to rein in some

control. “I hear sirens.”

"Let me know when the officer arrives."

"Okay." She took a deep breath. *Thank God, I live close to the police station.* She stood with her body flat against the wall for what seemed like forever. *Where are the police?* When the doorbell finally rang, she looked out her bedroom window, at a loss of what to do. *Will someone attack me if I go down?* The bell rang again and she descended the stairs with a tight grip on her stun gun. Through the plate-glass, she could see the dark uniform of the local police and with a sigh of relief she opened the door.

"The officer is here, thank you," she told the operator and hung up her phone.

The tall, balding officer stepped inside. "Please, stay here while I check your home."

Cammie nodded and moved aside, unable to loosen her grip on the stun gun. Her body still trembled at the thought of being violated.

Five minutes later, he came back into the foyer. "The house is clear. All your locks were engaged." He eyed her for a second. "Why don't you put that away and we'll do a quick walk-through so you can see what is missing?"

Cammie nodded and shoved the weapon into her back pocket. They walked through the rooms, one by one. Expensive electronics were in plain sight, only one thing was missing in the entire house. *Why?*

"The only thing missing is my mother's painting. It was over my bed." Her mouth went dry as she thought about her art studio in the back yard. "I have a studio out back full of my paintings."

The officer nodded. "Let's go check it out. How many people had a key to your house?"

"Just one...my housekeeper." She looked him in the

eyes. "I know she's not responsible for this."

Cammie followed him out her back door to a building about the size of a two-car garage. Opening the door, she could only stand and stare, heartbroken. Seven years of her artwork that had once decorated the walls was now scattered over the dark hardwood floors. Some canvases ripped, some unharmed but all tossed like garbage.

The officer looked around at the damage. "You should call your insurance company."

A tear slid down her face. "These are my work. But the real priceless piece of art was the one in my bedroom. It was my mother's and it can't be replaced."

"Maybe you could paint another one."

What part of priceless does he not understand? Impervious to her pain, he wrote a report and told her to have her locks changed as a precaution. After watching him drive away, she closed the door. *Why would someone want my mother's painting? It doesn't make any sense.*

*****

"Here's your new keys." The locksmith dropped the shiny pieces of metal into Cammie's palm.

She nodded and closed the wooden door behind him. As she stood in her foyer, she turned the pieces of silver over and over in her hand. Sighing, she traced the ridges of the new keys in her palm trying to get a grip on what had just happened. For a second time in her short twenty-two years, she'd been robbed of the most important thing in her life.

If she ever wanted to see the painting again, she would have to find out what happened to it herself. She had just gotten her PI license last month so she'd be her own first case. Determined to get back one of the only two things she had left to remember her mother, she stormed out of her back door with renewed energy.

The bronze doorknob lay on the counter where she had told the locksmith to leave it. Angry, she picked up the old knob and threw it across the room. If the monster that did this would've only damaged her art and not took her mother's painting she could deal. A tear slid down her face as she bent to pick up a butterfly picture that had been torn. She set the canvas back down and laughed like she had gone mad, then looked up to the ceiling. *Why does this stuff happen to me? What have I done to deserve so much loss?*

Since the age of fifteen, she had been using painting as a therapy of sorts to cope with her parents' sudden and tragic deaths. Her art studio was the only place she had felt truly at peace. *Will I ever feel at peace again?*

She looked around meticulously, hoping for some sort of clue then reached to pick up another painting on the floor when she saw a tiny, crumpled piece of a leaf. Hopeful, she picked up the narrow leaf and smoothed it out. *Why is this in here?* She studied the leaf and decided it definitely had not come from her yard. She wiped her watery eyes. This clue was going to get her mother's painting back someday. She didn't know how, but it would. After carefully placing the leaf piece inside her gold locket, she closed the door to her devastated studio.

*****

Cammie tried to get on with her day. If she'd learned anything, she knew life went on, no matter the tragedy.

She was still using a small office inside the front of her house for business and hadn't even managed to hire a secretary. When her housekeeper had offered to help with paperwork and messages Cammie was grateful. Nora was in her late forties and with her sugary personality close to that of Mary Poppins and Cammie adored her.

Nora stood with her hands clasped in front of her floral dress. "Would you like some more tea, Dear?"

Cammie looked up from her computer and shook her head.

Nora frowned. "Are you sure you don't want to talk more about what happened?"

"No. I'm okay, really." She paused. "You know, I will take some more tea."

Nora smiled and took her mug to the kitchen.

Cammie heard a knock at the front door, which was right outside her office. Nervous, she peeked out the window. A guy dressed in a tan uniform stood holding an envelope, so she went to open the door.

He looked at the white envelope in his hand. "Cammie Adams?"

She narrowed her eyes. "Yes."

"Great," he said, "this is for you."

I'm not expecting a delivery. "What is it?"

He blew out a breath. "Don't know." He looked down at his watch.

A bit suspicious, she took the envelope from him.

"Thanks," he said as he turned to go.

"Thank you." She closed the door and locked it.

The envelope had a simple white label with no return address. *Strange. Who is it from?* She went back into her office and sat down on her leather chair. When she opened the envelope, she found a handwritten letter. Her hands shook as she began to read. If she had known whom the letter was from she never would have opened it and guessed her aunt knew that as well. She didn't want to continue, but something made her keep reading.

Cammie,
I hope this letter finds its way to you in time. I am sorry for the way that I treated you. There were reasons I could not explain. I guess you are wondering why I decided to contact you after all these years. I know I have no right to ask you for anything. I am in trouble. You may have something that can help me. I can't explain in this letter. I really need to talk to you and hope you can find it in your heart to forgive me. Again, I am sorry. My phone number is on the back of this letter if you choose to get in contact with me.
Yours,
Eve

Anger rose inside her. She wiped away her tears and dried her face, then went to find Nora in the kitchen. *This is turning into a really crappy day.*

She tried to control the fury in her voice. "I have to leave."

"Is everything alright, Dear?" Nora asked.

"Yes, you can take the rest of the day off."

Nora frowned. "Is there anything I can do?"

She forced a smile. "No, something's just come up."

Nora nodded and got her purse.

Too many strange things were happening and she didn't want Nora caught in the middle. She needed to clear her head. She put on her running shoes and tucked her gold locket under her T-shirt. *Why did my aunt contact me? Did she steal my mother's painting? No, that would be ridiculous.* She had thought once she got into that taxi, all those years ago, she would never have to deal with Eve again.

As Cammie jogged through her Northern California community, Brandywine Estates, she let her mind take her back to that horrific day. It had all happened so fast. Her parents were going on vacation, but they never got to Greece because their small plane crashed into the Atlantic Ocean. Their bodies were never recovered. Right after the memorial, her Aunt Eve sent her to live at The Kipton Hotel with her inheritance. She had never felt so lost and alone.

*****

The next morning, when the sunlight hit her face, Cammie wondered if the robbery and the letter from her aunt had just been a nightmare. She rubbed her eyes, looked over at the nightstand and saw the letter right where she'd left it. *Damn, it was all real.* Frowning, she got up and got dressed to run.

After a few quick stretches, she jogged around some small puddles left over from the storm last night. When she rounded a curve, she heard a car coming up close behind. She turned her head to look and saw a black Town Car. The car quickly stopped beside her. An eerie feeling came over her as she reached for her phone. A man wearing a dark suit and sunglasses got out of the car and grabbed her before she could dial. She struggled to free herself from his strong grasp. A needle pricked her neck and the blackness closed in.

*****

Simon Fisher looked at his best friend and mentor with assurance. *This would be the most important job they would ever do together.* He wished Max were as confident as he was. Simon would love to get a hold of that ruby, but the mission this time, wasn't about the jewel.

Max smiled and ran his fingers through his hair, "She really is my princess. You will keep her safe, right?"

Simon knew of the princess types and it usually only meant one thing...spoiled. He would have to protect Max's spoiled-rotten daughter with his own life and he would do it without question. He owed Max everything.

Simon nodded. "Yes, you have my word."

Max shook his hand. "The jet is fired up and ready. They would have taken her to Greece, you know the place."

His friend turned to go downstairs. Simon looked down at the old picture of Cammie in his hand and shook his head. He had never put a woman before jewels in his life.

Simon went downstairs and grabbed his bags, then threw them in the taxi's trunk, Max had called for him. He glanced out the window as the car drove away. He wasn't worried, because he knew he could get Cammie out and on the jet before the abductors even realized she was gone. After all, his skills had once made him a successful, jewel thief. Max had put Simon's skills to different use when he hired him as his bodyguard. Now he would become Cammie's protector until this was over. *Hopefully, Miss Priss isn't too high maintenance.*

Simon thought back to the meeting that had prompted

his journey. Cammie's aunt, Eve, had called Max in a panic. She said she had been followed. By the time Simon went to check on Cammie, it was too late. He looked again at the picture of the fifteen-year-old girl with long blonde hair and wide blue eyes too big for her face. Max had told him the photo was taken seven years ago. That would make her twenty-two now, just six years younger than him. With determination, he folded the picture and put it into his back pocket.

*****

Cammie's head hurt like she had been out all night drinking, though she hadn't had a drop of alcohol. Her recollection was a little fuzzy. Panic overcame her when she opened her eyes. She tried to focus, but the room was too dark. Slowly her memory started to return. *The car, the man wearing sunglasses and darkness. Oh God.* She felt for her cell phone... he must have taken it.

She gasped and felt for her locket. It was still there tucked under her shirt. *Thank goodness.* Her mother had given her the locket right before she left. She'd made Cammie promise to never take it off.

Dizzy, she got up from what felt like a futon mattress. Hoping to find a light switch, she felt along the walls. *Nothing.* Judging from the number of steps, the room was about as big as her art studio. There wasn't any furniture except for the mattress. The door to the room opened, light spilled in from the hallway. She jumped when a man walked into the room.

"Be a good girl and you will live," the man spoke in an unfamiliar accent.

Wearing a tight, polyester jumpsuit, he looked to be in

his fifties. *Not the same man who grabbed me. Crap, there is more than one abductor.* Her chances of escaping were slim.

Fear caught her breath. "Please, let me go."

He looked like he could overpower her even if she tried to make a run for it.

"My boss wants what is rightfully his." His English was good, though his accent was thick.

Cammie's hands shook. "There must be a mistake. I don't have anything. Please let me go." *Nothing is making sense. First my mother's painting was stolen, then the strange letter from Eve, now this. Are all these crazy things connected?*

"You cooperate, you go back home, just relax." He set down a bag. "Eat, you must be getting hungry. We will talk later." He left the room and locked the door.

Within seconds, a light turned on from above. She looked up to a ceiling light about fifteen feet high. The smell of the food made her eyes move down to the bag on the stained cement floor. Her stomach growled. It felt like she hadn't eaten in days. *How long has it been*? *Impossible to tell what time of day it is without windows.*

She needed strength if she were going to escape. He'd said she would be unharmed if she cooperated. *Was he telling the truth?* She walked over to the bag and peeked inside, Chinese take-out and a bottle of water. Hesitant, she opened the white container to smell the food. *Smells okay. Still, it could be poisoned.*

She decided to try just a couple of bites. The warm shrimp and rice tasted good. After three bites, she started to close it back up, but her stomach continued its protest so she finished the meal. Now with adequate nutrition, she could think of how to get away from him.

Who could his boss be? What could he think I have that belongs to him? She had to find a way out of this room. It seemed like hours passed as she tried to think of a way to escape.

The light went off making Cammie's heart skip a beat. The man came into the room and had her in handcuffs before she knew what happened. The light came back on causing her blink.

"Let's go." He pulled on her.

She tried to be brave. "Just tell me what you want so I can get back home to my husband. I'm sure he's called the police by now," she lied, looking him in his sunglass-covered eyes. *Maybe if he thinks I'm married, he'll think someone is looking for me. Hopefully, Nora will realize something isn't right.*

"If only it were that simple. I will explain later. We have a flight to catch." He grasped her arm and pulled her toward the door.

Cammie gasped and shook her head backing away. Nothing he could have done to her would be much worse than making her get on a plane.

"I can't fly. Please, can't we take a train or bus or a boat? I can't get on a plane." Her mouth went dry and her hands shook.

He took a blindfold out of his pocket before opening the door. "We must fly."

She screamed as loud as she could and tried to bite him when he put the blindfold over her eyes.

"You do not want to go to sleep like you did before do you?"

Cammie shook her head feeling dizzy.

"Good girl. Screaming will do you no good. We are flying on a private plane."

She couldn't see anything through the thick cloth, so she counted her steps to try and figure out where she was. The walk was straight and too long for a house. Their footsteps echoed a bit. She could hear an extra set of footsteps. *Maybe the pilot or the person who turned on the light?* After about a hundred steps, she heard what sounded like a huge garage door opening. *A warehouse of some kind? Does Nora know I'm missing yet? Maybe she called the police.*

Cammie realized she was outside when she felt the breeze on her face and heard an engine roar to life. They walked another fifty paces, then took ten steps up. She tried to think about Nora and her best friends Dinah and Miles. She tried to think about anything other than the horrifying plane.

Rough hands pushed her down in a seat and buckled her in. When he removed her blindfold, his sunglasses were off. *Jumpsuit guy. Where is suit guy? The pilot maybe?* Sitting in the seat next to hers, his dark wrinkled eyes looked at her with curiosity. She looked out the window to find it was dark outside.

She turned to look back at him. "Where are we going?"

"You will find out when we arrive. It will be a long flight. Might as well get some rest."

She looked at him in disbelief. *He thinks I can sleep when my life is at stake?* Maybe she could escape before the plane took off. She lifted her hands. "Can I at least get these handcuffs off? They're hurting my wrists."

He studied her face. "Not yet. When we arrive at our destination and I have explained why we are there, I may un-cuff you. Have a drink... try to relax." He handed her a bottle of rum.

Cammie reached for the bottle with her cuffed hands.

Because she was terrified of flying, she tilted the bottle to her lips. *Not again!* The blackness closed in.

Chapter Two

Simon slipped unnoticed through the old, stone building avoiding the two guards watching TV downstairs. Dressed in black from head to toe and fitted with night vision infrared goggles, he slipped up the curved stairs like an invisible fox. Of the five rooms upstairs, only one was locked. With steady expert hands, he opened the lock with ease. He immediately saw Cammie lying limp on an old mattress, the only thing between her and the dirty floor.

Simon bent down to put his fingers on her neck, relieved when he found she still had a strong pulse. *They must have sedated her. Just as well, I can get her out faster without having to explain.* Simon scooped up Cammie, carried her down the stairs and out the window that he pried open ten minutes earlier. He flung her over his shoulder and closed the window behind him. The guards probably wouldn't even check on her until morning. That would buy him some time.

After carrying her a few blocks down the back streets, he was thankful she wasn't heavy. When he arrived at the hotel, he pulled off his black mask and shook his hair back into place. He used his key card to enter the hotel from the back entrance. A middle-aged man walked down the hall as Simon was carrying Cammie to their room.

Simon shrugged. "My wife, too much to drink," he said to the man as he passed.

The man nodded and gave him a look of understanding.

When he got her back to the room, he carefully laid her on the bed and looked down at her. She'd been unconscious through the whole rescue. Maybe he should take her to the hospital. *What if she is in a coma?* She looked different from the picture he had inside his pocket. He admired her curvaceous hips and full lips. *Without a doubt, she is a woman now. So much for the teenager I had pictured.*

He needed to get her some food. It would help get the drugs out of her system. He had always loved stealing jewels because of the rush it gave him. He had gotten a rush when he scooped Cammie up in his arms, but not the kind of rush he had ever experienced.

When he lifted her up and felt the warmth of her skin and her soft hair brushing against his face, he knew he would protect her, no matter what. Max's daughter would be safe. He wouldn't let anyone hurt her. He disabled the phone and hid the supplies, precautions in case she woke up before he could get back.

*****

Cammie woke up once again with a headache, not knowing where she was or how she got there. She sat up from the bed, inside a small hotel room. She tried the door and found it locked. Tired and afraid, she looked out the small round window. *Damn, too small to climb out.* The view was of the ocean and colorful buildings stacked upon a hillside. She saw a phone on the bedside table and picked it up, no dial tone. After she made sure it was plugged in, she bit her lip. She started to scream, but remembered his warning. *How many people are in on this? What do they want with me?* Glancing out the window again, she guessed the room was at least a few stories high.

Cammie looked down at her hands. She had almost forgotten she had handcuffs on in the plane. They must have taken them off when they put her here. *Where is here?* Anyplace was better than a plane. She would do as her abductor said for now. Maybe if he was telling the truth he would let her go soon, when he found out she didn't have anything that belonged to his boss.

She heard the door handle rattle and froze. The door opened. A guy in his late twenties dressed in a tight-fitting, white T-shirt and dark jeans walked into the room carrying a small paper bag. He had wavy dark-brown hair that fell just over his ears and a five o' clock shadow. His brown hazel eyes were surprisingly kind. He didn't look like an abductor. *How can someone so hot be life threatening? Great! Now I'm attracted to some psycho.*

"Good, you're awake. I was starting to think I should've taken you to the hospital. You're safe now. They don't know where you are." He reached into the bag removing a takeout box she didn't recognize. "Here have something to eat."

Cammie looked at him confused. *Why is he acting like he rescued me?* "Who are you? What's going on?" she whispered.

"My name is Simon Fisher. I'm here to keep you safe from the men that took you."

She narrowed her eyes, confused. "What? You're not one of them?"

"Not hardly. Just eat and I'll explain." Simon pushed the food toward her.

"What *is* it with you people giving me food? I eat. I pass out. I wake up. This *has* to stop! I will not take one more bite or drink of *anything*, until I get some answers." She didn't know where the sudden courage came from, but enough was enough. She had to find out why she was here and more importantly when she could go back home.

"Okay, Cammie. I'll give you answers. But listen without interrupting, because I have a lot to tell you and we're in a hurry."

"How do you know my name?" she asked, surprised.

He shook his head and sighed. "Interrupting."

She took a deep breath, nodded and waited for him to go on.

"I just rescued you from some very dangerous men. I'm a friend of your father, Max. Your parents led a different life before you were born. The fact is... they were jewel thieves."

Her mouth fell open, but she didn't speak. *He's a liar.*

"When you were fifteen, the people they had stolen a ruby from before you were born, somehow found out who they were." He rubbed his scruffy face. "They hadn't given up looking for that ruby and wanted it back at any cost. Word got back to your parents that they were no longer safe." He paused to look at her. "When your parents were on their way to Greece a plane did crash, however your parents weren't on it. They staged the crash to protect you." He paused. "Your father's alive."

Her heart raced. "My parents are alive?"

"Your father is. Your mother however, was killed. I've been told she was a very brave woman." He sat next to her and put his hands on his knees. "Your parents had to fake their deaths to protect you. Hired thugs caught up to them on their way out of the country. They thought your parents had the ruby on them. There was a struggle, your father managed to escape with only a bullet wound. Your mother wasn't so lucky."

Cammie shook her head in disbelief. "Why didn't they just give the ruby back?"

"Your parents had made it so only you would be able to retrieve the ruby once you turned twenty-two."

She bit her lip. "If I get the ruby my father will be safe?"

"Yes. After all, those men are responsible for your mother's death. They know your father has that on them. Will you help your father?"

"How do I know you're telling me the truth? How do I know you're not one of the bad guys?" Cammie looked at him trying to keep her emotions in check. She desperately wanted to believe her father was alive, jewel thief or not.

"Your father told me you were smart. Okay, here's something only he would know. On your eleventh birthday, when you fell off your new skateboard, he told your mother they should've gotten you the art set instead. You have a scar on your left ankle from the fall."

Without thinking, she jumped and grabbed Simon's arms. "My father's alive!" Realizing what she had done, she blushed and quickly let go of him. Then reality hit her that her mother was still gone. "My mother was murdered?" Cammie looked down to hide unshed tears that stung her eyes.

Simon looked at her with sympathy. "Your mother loved what she was doing and knew the risks. She gave it up to keep you safe. Everything would've been fine if the man they stole the ruby from didn't track them down."

She let his words sink in and realized she could die. "What if I –"

He cut her off, "You won't. I'm the best at what I do.

You are completely safe with me. If you weren't, your father would have never asked this of you."

She nodded in agreement. "Of course he wouldn't." She paused. "Where are we?"

"Greece. Max asked me to tell you how very sorry he is. He loves you and wants so much to see you when it's safe."

My whole childhood was a lie? Odd bits and pieces had all pointed to the truth. Her parents had a safe behind their bedroom mirror, which held her mother's jewelry box filled with elaborate necklaces and bracelets Cammie had assumed were costume jewelry. Her mother would only let her try on the jewels when no one else was around. And the painting. The truth had been right in front of her all along. Cammie looked down at her chest and grabbed a hold of the locket her mother told her to never take off.

"Can I contact my housekeeper to let her know I'm okay?" She didn't want to tell him she was a PI. He knew enough about her already.

He smirk danced over his lips. "Your housekeeper?"

"She's more than a housekeeper. She's a dear friend."

He shook his head. "Not a good idea. No one can know what you are doing or about the ruby. If you called her how would you explain?"

She rubbed her dry lips together. "I hate this. I don't want her thinking I'm dead. How long will this take?"

He looked at her and hesitated. "It may take a couple weeks."

Cammie shook her head. "I have to let her know that I'm alive. That's the only way I can do this."

Simon took a deep breath. "Let me think." He stood up and paced around the room.

"I really want my father back more than anything." She walked over to the small window.

Simon nodded and went over to the phone, unscrewed something and snapped it back together. He dialed a number and spoke Greek, so she had no idea what he was saying.

When he hung up the phone, she asked, "Won't it be a problem that I don't speak Greek?"

Simon looked at her and replied, "Good question, but no. It's not a problem because we're not staying here long."

She sat down on the bed feeling faint. "Where's my father?"

"He's safe."

"Where's the ruby?"

Simon raked his fingers through his hair. "In a safe deposit box, back in the states. It can only be opened with your finger print and account number."

What? "But I don't know the account number."

"Your father told me your mother gave you something before they left. She told you to keep it on you at all times."

Her hand immediately went to her necklace. "She gave me this locket. But it just has a picture of her and my father inside."

"Can I see it?" Simon held out his hand.

She reluctantly took off the necklace and opened it, then slipped the leaf into her pocket and handed it to him. If he noticed she took something out of it, he didn't say.

He looked inside. "Trust me." He took a tiny tool out of his pocket and gently slipped out both pictures. Cammie stood up next to him to see what he was doing, smelling a mix of spicy-cinnamon and citrus. The scent was so seductive she stepped away to break the spell it was putting on her. *What is wrong with me? This is no time for my hormones to suddenly kick in.* He held the locket up to his face and studied it.

"Here, engraved into the gold. Put the left and right side numbers together and you have your full account number." He showed her, then carefully put the pictures back into place, closed it and handed it back to her. "Do as your mother instructed and keep it on at all times. Putting the number inside something she knew you would hang onto without having to explain, was genius."

Should I trust him? "I'm not sure if this is important, but there is something that I need to tell you about my Aunt Eve."

"Let me guess, she tried to contact you?"

Cammie drew her eyebrows together. "Yes, she wrote me a letter, said I had something she needed." *Should I tell him about the stolen painting?* She wanted to trust him. Something about his eyes told her she could.

"Your father said that your aunt didn't want to go through with their plan. Your parents had to convince her that your lives were at stake. The thugs who took you, now have your aunt. They were looking for the ruby. I have to go rescue her."

"Okay, but how?" The question felt so weird coming out of her mouth when up until now she had hated her aunt with a passion.

"You'll stay here and I'll go get her," Simon said.

Reality of the situation suddenly hit her. "I don't know if I can do this, my father's a criminal. For all I know, so are you." Cammie went into the bathroom and shut the door. *This is too much, too fast.* She had always wished for her parents to somehow be alive, always hoped the accident was a mistake. When she was younger she had fantasized so many times about them being alive. Never in her wildest dreams did she imagine these circumstances.

Her parents had made a living off of stolen jewels. Her mother's death was not an accident. Though she always wondered. One of the reasons she became a PI... to find truths in a world of lies and secrets.

She sat on the edge of the tub with her hands over her face. So many questions raced through her mind. She wanted to be angry with her father and run back home, but she couldn't. No matter what her parents had done, she knew that they were good people. They always made her feel loved and cared for. She wouldn't let this ruin her memories of them. Family was the most important thing. She would stick by her father no matter what.

*****

Simon sighed and looked at the closed door. He had expected her to whine, he hadn't expected her to cry. He hated when women cried. When he walked into the room and saw those big, blue eyes, something stirred deep inside him. She was pretty enough when she was sleeping, but awake she was...intriguing. *Maybe this wasn't such a good idea. Maybe Max can get the ruby another way. Women are only dangerous if you let them get too close*. He had keeping women at a safe distance, down to an art. *Stopping now would just be stupid.*

*****

Cammie wiped her eyes and stood up when she heard three quick knocks on the door.

"You're free to go. In fact, I'll take you home myself," Simon called through the barrier separating them.

She opened the door as he was walking away. "I'm okay now. I appreciate all you have done for my family. I shouldn't have judged you."

"Understandable. You have a safe, ordinary life. That's enough for some people. But others, we need the thrill, I guess." Simon smiled a smile that would probably make most women melt.

What would make someone become a jewel thief and risk everything else? "You love the thrill. What about a normal life?"

"I've come close to normal before, but not enough to become a punch-the-clock kind of guy in a boring suburban community." He reached into his pocket and pulled out a cheap cell phone. "About your housekeeper, if you don't say anything about where you are or why, you could give her a quick phone call. You can tell her anything except the truth."

"Can I tell her I'm helping my aunt? That's probably the only way she'll be satisfied enough not to call the police."

"Just be careful. All of our lives are at stake if she suspects anything."

Cammie nodded and whispered, "Okay."

"Make it quick." He handed her the phone.

She took a deep breath and dialed Nora's cell.

"Hello?" Nora answered.

"Nora–"

"Cammie, is that you?" She could hear panic in her voice.

"Yes, it's me. I'm okay."

"Where are you?"

"I can't explain now. I had to help my Aunt Eve with something important. If Dinah or Miles call, please tell them I'll be gone for a while. Don't worry about the other thing we were working on. Just let that line go straight to voicemail."

"Are you sure you're okay, Dear?"

Cammie swallowed her terror down. "I'll explain everything when I get back." Simon motioned for her to wrap it up. "I have to go."

She handed Simon the phone and he stomped it to pieces.

Her legs felt wobbly like she might faint, so she went over to the bed to sit down.

Simon went over to her and awkwardly patted her back. "You okay?"

She let him comfort her for a few seconds, then stood up. "Let's just do this so my father will be safe."

Simon nodded. "Your aunt is being kept prisoner here." He pointed to a roughly sketched map he'd drawn out on a notepad. "There are a couple of men guarding the house where she's being held. You will have to stay inside this hotel room so you're not spotted."

After he folded up the paper and put it in his pocket, he walked over to the window.

Cammie wiped her sweaty palms on her shorts. "The men who took me and now have my aunt, are they still looking for me?"

Simon stood, peering out the small window. "If they've realized you're gone, they're looking. You're safe here, for now. We just have to make sure we get your aunt and get out of Greece before they find us."

She walked over to where he was standing. He moved over and she looked out to the sea with him.

"Nice view. Too bad we're not on vacation." Cammie rolled her eyes.

Simon laughed. "Don't worry. I'll get you through this."

"What if they find me while you're gone? I'll feel like a sitting duck here."

"I won't be long. Maybe an hour tops."

She looked into his hazel eyes, more brown than green at the moment. "What if I came with you?"

Simon smirked. "Uh, not such a good idea. I've already rescued you once, remember?"

"Maybe I can help. I can be your lookout or something."

He studied her face as if to see if she was serious. "You're a lot tougher than I imagined."

"I'm terrified, but I don't want to stay here by myself."

He thought for a minute. "I don't know. It could be risky."

She paused. "I could wear a disguise."

Simon sighed. "Okay, we'll wait until the sun is about to go down. There is a shop across the street. We can get you and your aunt some sunglasses and scarves to help hide your faces."

She nodded. "So what do I do?"

He ran his fingers through his hair. "You can be my lookout. I have some supplies inside the nightstand." He opened the door to reveal a small black duffel bag. He took out the items and placed them on the bed. "This is a communication device that fits inside your ear. And these night vision infrared binoculars will let you see me from far away even in the dark."

Cammie looked at him with eyes wide, then at the tiny earpiece and small binoculars. She had no idea spy gear really existed, let alone knew how to use it.

A sly smile crossed his lips. “It’s okay, I’ll show you.”

Chapter Three

Cammie gripped Simon's strong, but surprisingly soft hand as they walked through the hotel. She felt safer with his confident grip. The hotel was nice, but not as luxurious as her friend Miles' hotel, The Kipton. She tried to be brave. *This has to work.* For the first time in her life, she was worried about her Aunt Eve. Now that she knew that her aunt had only been protecting her and following her parents' wishes, it changed everything.

More determined than afraid, she walked through the lobby wearing a hat with her hair tucked underneath and a dress at least two sizes too big, Simon had *borrowed* from a lady in a random hotel room. The dress was so baggy she just left her shirt and shorts on underneath. She kept her head down as they passed the hotel employees. Simon had convinced her they should appear as a couple vacationing to blend in with the other tourists.

The street was busy giving them opportunity to blend in the crowd. They crossed the road to the little tourist shop. Simon opened the door for her. Cammie walked inside, went to a rack and quickly chose two scarves. He paid for the merchandise. Cammie's heart pounded as a man walked toward them, then let out a sigh of relief when he walked right by. She took the yellow scarf from Simon and wrapped the silk fabric around her head to cover as much of her face as possible. After Simon nodded his approval, they walked out the door and he took her hand again as they made their way down the street.

Once they turned down a side street, the voices from the crowd faded.

"You're going to be my lookout. I'll be in and out with Eve, within fifteen minutes. Put these on and we will be able to hear each other," he said, handing her the earpiece. "You'll be sitting across the street on a bench. You will be able to see everything from your location with these." He gave her the spy binoculars. "If things don't go as planned, no matter what go back to the hotel. Here is my pilot's number, call him and he will get you back home." Simon assured her with his confident smile. "No worries, though, that's a huge if. We'll be fine."

Is this really happening? "We have to be. I'm ready."

"Do we need to go over the plan once more?" Simon asked, leading her down the street.

"No." This was the first she'd seen of Greece other than out the tiny window of the hotel room. It was dusk, but she could still make out the colors of the ancient white-washed-limestone, stacked buildings with their orange tiled roofs. She wished that she *were* here on vacation. When Simon stopped at a bench in front of a small restaurant, she knew they'd arrived at their destination. Simon sat down next to her, took the blue scarf and shoved it into his pocket.

He whispered in her ear, "You see that building across the street?"

She looked. "Yes."

"Eve's inside. I'm going to get her and bring her to you, okay?"

"Okay." She grabbed his arm. "Please be careful."

"Stay here. Keep your face covered. If anyone tries to

grab you, scream. People inside the restaurant will hear you."

Cammie swallowed hard. *Maybe I should have stayed in the hotel room.*

"Ready?"

She nodded. "Ready."

Simon got up and walked down the street, then cut across toward the building. When she saw him disappear, her stomach fell.

"Can you hear me, Cammie?" Simon's voice came through the earpiece so loud it made her jump.

"Yes."

"Good, I'm going in."

She slid down her scarf a bit and peeked out with the tiny binoculars. An armed man was standing on the left side of the building. He started walking around back. "Wait! There's a guy outside walking toward the back."

"Okay." The same man walked back to the front and looked around for a moment, then he leaned on the side of the building and lit a cigarette. "All clear Simon, he's smoking."

"Got it." All went quiet. She waited and watched.

After about ten minutes, she started to worry. She hadn't seen any sign of Simon. *What is taking so long? What if they captured him?*

"I have her," Simon's voice whispered in her earpiece.

Moments later, Simon and her aunt came running down the street toward her. Cammie stood up and rushed to meet them.

"Let's move ladies, as fast as you can without running. Eve, stay right behind us. No talking until we get inside the hotel room." Simon took a hold of Cammie's hand when they reached the busy street of the hotel.

When they got into the room, Simon started wiping it down for prints. "We have to get out of here before they realize their second prisoner is missing. You two make sure you don't leave anything behind."

Eve pulled Cammie into a tight embrace. "I'm so sorry."

She hugged Eve back. "I know. I understand now."

"Simon told me that Elizabeth was murdered. I warned Max something like that would happen," Eve told her with tears in her eyes.

"It's not my father's fault. My mother would want us to focus on saving him. She would want us to put this to an end. We have to be strong."

"You've become such a smart, brave woman. You remind me so much of her, you know."

Cammie smiled. "Thank you, that means a lot."

"Ladies, sorry to cut the reunion short, but we have a jet to catch," Simon told them. "We need to get out of Greece now."

Cammie closed her eyes. "Not again, I hate flying."

Eve took her hand. "Me too, but we can do this together."

Simon turned to Eve. "Follow a foot behind us, keep your head down."

Eve nodded.

Simon and Cammie walked out of the hotel. Eve followed behind them as instructed. Simon called the pilot and told him they were ready to go. He hailed a taxi that drove them to the private jet. Cammie closed her eyes and her stomach dropped at the thought of flying.

Simon looked at Cammie. "Are you okay?"

No! "I will be, when all this is over."

They got to the jet as it was about to take off. Cammie tried not to look out the window as the jet rose into the air leaving the ground far behind them. Eve removed her scarf revealing short, blonde ringlets and one single freckle under her nose. The single freckle gene must have run in the family. Cammie's mother had one on her forehead and Cammie had one on her cheek.

Eve took Cammie's hand. "Tell me about your life. Tell me what I have missed."

Cammie started from the day she last saw her aunt. "A boy my age worked at his grandfather's hotel and we became quick friends. Miles has always been there for me."

Eve smiled. "I'm glad you had someone."

"As we got older Miles loved me in a different way than I did him. He asked me to marry him, but I couldn't. He was like a brother to me. I've felt guilty ever since, wishing I could give him what he wanted."

"You've been through so much."

Cammie sighed. "It hasn't been easy." She took a drink of bottled water. "Dinah is my other friend. She's married and has a little boy."

"What about you? Have you found anyone special?"

Cammie shook her head. "I'm broken, Aunt Eve. I'm not in any shape to be in a relationship."

Eve squeezed her eyes shut and then opened them. "Oh honey, I'm so sorry."

"Don't feel sorry for me. I've managed." She paused. "How about you? Do you have someone?"

Eve laughed. "Someone, no. A career, yes."

Cammie sat up in her seat remembering her own career that she hadn't really even started yet. "So, what is your career?"

"You are looking at the Senior Editor for Modern Home Magazine."

Cammie smiled. “Why couldn’t my mother have picked an honest career like yours?”
Eve moved a stray curl out of her eyes. “I’m sorry you had to grow up without a mother.”
Cammie yawned as her eyelids got heavy. “My housekeeper, Nora has been a great mother figure.”

*****

Things were going smoothly. Both women were safe. Max would be pleased his plan was working. Simon glanced up at Cammie. He learned more than he cared to by overhearing their conversation. *Maybe I was wrong about her. She doesn’t seem spoiled at all.* She had actually surprised him, but he could have done without the emotion… something he wasn’t wholly comfortable with.
He had to fight whatever was inside him that made him want to kiss those soft, full lips of hers. Besides, he could never get involved with Max’s daughter. He had always had his choice of women. And he had always known when to move on. Some women just needed more than he could give them and he was pretty sure Cammie was one of those women.

*****

“We’re here ladies,” Simon said, waking up Cammie and Eve. “We have to get Eve into hiding until the ruby is back in place.”
Cammie climbed out of the jet so happy to see land. “I guess flying isn’t so bad once you get over the fear of crashing.”

Eve smiled. "Yeah and sleeping helps, too."

They climbed into the taxi waiting for them. Simon sat in the middle. Cammie could smell his cologne, which made her uneasy. She was surprised she felt so close to her aunt who she had hated yesterday.

As if Eve were reading her mind she said, "It won't be long. We'll have the rest of our lives. I can't wait to meet Nora, Dinah and Miles."

Cammie sighed. "I know. It just feels like so much time has been wasted already."

When they were in the vicinity of Eve's hide out, Simon told the driver to stop the car and he paid him. They got out and walked about a mile to an old farmhouse with peeling paint and shutters that were falling off. He unlocked the door. They went inside and Cammie's mouth fell open. It looked totally different inside with freshly painted walls. The furnishings and the hard wood floors were high quality.

Simon smiled. "Surprised?"

"It looks abandoned from the outside," Cammie replied.

"Good, that's the idea. Eve you'll be safe here. The house is stocked with food, clothes, even a secure laptop. You should have everything you need until this is over. Max knew you would want your own place until you guys could work things out. There just isn't enough time to do that right now."

"Of course. We do have a lot to work out, but that can wait until later," Eve said.

"Cammie, there are lots of extra clothes stashed here. I got a few different sizes so hopefully something will fit."

Cammie went through the clothes, looking for her size. She found a few and stuffed them into a duffel bag. Her aunt wasn't the cold-hearted witch she'd thought. All this time she could have had family.

"Okay," Eve said and hugged her. "I'll see you soon. Go save your father so we can finally put an end to this."

"I will. Be safe," Cammie replied hugging her back.

Before leaving, Cammie and Simon changed their clothes. They walked out back to an old garage. Simon opened the door to reveal a black sports car inside.

"Why am I not surprised?" Cammie said, getting into the Corvette.

He winked. "You're a fast learner."

"Where are we going now?"

He looked over at her. "Getting something to eat. I'm starving, aren't you?"

She fastened her seatbelt. "Yeah, actually. How soon can we get the ruby?"

"We'll stop at a motel to rest. First thing in the morning, when the bank opens you can go retrieve your ruby."

She watched the farmhouse disappear in the rear view mirror. "My ruby, why did my parents think I had to have a ruby? Didn't they know all I needed was their love? If they wouldn't have taken it, everything would be so different."

"I'm sure they did what they thought was right at the time. Things happen for a reason. We can't change who we are or how we got here."

All the lies, all the heartache. Why? "I always blamed myself. I thought that if I had told them not to go, they wouldn't have been on that plane. To find out it was all a lie –"

He stopped her. "Everything will work out. You'll see."

She sighed. "I hope so. I really do."

"Let's grab a burger and fries." Simon pulled up to a drive thru. He ordered cheeseburgers, fries and large chocolate shakes. He handed Cammie the sack of food and pulled the car over so they could eat.

"I normally don't eat this stuff," Cammie said, taking out the greasy food.

Simon slurped his shake. "Really? You're missing out."

"Do you always do things that are bad for you? Eating bad foods, rescuing women from men with guns?"

He grinned. "Yeah, pretty much. Living on the edge is invigorating. You should try it sometime."

Cammie shook her head. "No, I like safe and legal."

"That's because you're afraid to let that part of yourself out. Adventure's in your blood. Both of your parents loved what they did. I think you're more like your mother than you know." *Maybe he is partly right.* She did choose to become a PI instead of a professional artist.

She wiped her salty fingers on a napkin. "I am like her, but not in the way you're thinking. I knew her as a very nurturing caring person. I still miss her."

"I'm sorry."

They finished eating in companionable silence. Simon took their trash and dumped it in the parking trashcan.

"How much longer until we get to the motel?" Cammie asked when he got back inside.

He glanced at the digital clock. "About an hour."

"If you don't mind my asking, were you ever in the, um, jewel business?"

He smirked. "Used to be."

"How'd you meet my father anyway?" she asked.

"Remember when I told you things aren't always what they seem?"

"Yeah."

"I could tell you, but then I'd have to kill you and that would defeat the purpose of me saving you." He winked.

She rolled her eyes. "Never mind, I don't even want to know."

"Yeah you do or you wouldn't have asked." He smirked.

"Just trying to make conversation."

He turned the car right at the light. "It's simple really, I'm a bodyguard now."

Jewel thief to bodyguard. This man is full of surprises. "A bodyguard?"

He glanced over at her. "Yes, yours to be specific."

What? "You're kidding right?"

He shook his head. "Afraid not, your father hired me."

Of course he did. "What made you go from a jewel thief to a bodyguard?"

"Back to living on the edge. Working for your father has been as living on the edge as it gets."

She should probably be scared of this guy, but for some crazy reason she wasn't. "Were you anyone else's bodyguard before mine?"

"Your father's up until he asked me to start protecting *you*."

Cammie thought for a second. "You told me that you were the best and would never get caught. Why do I need a bodyguard?"

"Just a precaution. You have a protective father."

She crossed her arms. "Maybe if my father would stop trying to protect me so much, we wouldn't be in this mess."

He shrugged. "Afraid you'll have to take that up with him. I'm just the bodyguard."

It was getting dark. Cammie stared out her window and

tried to process everything that had happened to her in the past week. She was afraid to go to sleep, because maybe this was all just a dream and she'd wake up to find her father still dead.

She looked over at Simon, so self-confident, it was hard not to be attracted to him. "So after I'm back home, who will you protect?"

"I haven't given it much thought. I'm only concerned with this job right now." Simon pulled into a drug store parking lot. He parked the car and looked at her. "I figure you probably need some girly things."

"Thank you." *I can get lip-gloss! And a brush, I must look like crap.*

"Get whatever you need. You better grab a handbag so you'll have one to take to the bank."

They walked inside and went in separate directions. Cammie headed toward the make-up. With a laugh, she realized she'd never owned a handbag from a CVS. She grabbed a small, black vinyl handbag and frowned recalling her Coach purse at home. She took a plastic shopping basket and threw in a toothbrush, toothpaste, deodorant, soap, shampoo, conditioner, razor, shaving cream, brush, eye shadow, lip-gloss and a cold bottle of sweet tea. *Shopping, no matter where or why is still shopping.* Simon had a toothbrush and deodorant when they reached the checkout.

He looked at her full basket and laughed. "Not too bad for a girl, I guess."

She rolled her eyes, then blushed looking at his two items. Simon grabbed an extra bottle of sweet tea, paid for their stuff and they got back into the car. About ten minutes later, they arrived at Riverside Motel. Simon turned off the car and grabbed their duffel bag that held the extra clothes.

Cammie groaned. "Please tell me this is another farm house situation."

"Sorry, this time things *are* what they seem."

She looked at the cheap motel in front of her and realized she had never stayed in a dump like this before. *It's only one night.* Simon checked in and got their key. He opened the door and asked which bed she wanted.

This could get awkward. "I'll take the one closest to the bathroom."

"Great, I guess the one by the window is mine," Simon said, flopping down.

Cammie was still fighting sleep. "Are you tired? Because I could stay up a while."

"I could stay up for a while, too. Do you mind if I take off my shirt?" Simon asked.

She shrugged ignoring her raging hormones. "Why would I mind?"

"Just trying to being polite." Simon took off his shirt.

She tried not to look. *Too late. Wow, his stomach is ripped. Hard to believe after what he had just eaten.* Cammie quickly looked away embarrassed.

"So do you think I'll run into any problems at the bank?" she asked.

He leaned on his bed with his head propped up. "Nope. You have the account number and your fingerprint."

"So how big *is* this ruby?"

A sly smile spread across his gorgeous face. "Big enough. Do you want to know how much it's worth?"

"No. I don't care. It doesn't matter. I just wanted to know what to expect when I opened the safe deposit box." She paused. "So what happens after we have the ruby? Will I get to see my father?"

"After you get the ruby we'll stay at his place while he goes to Greece to return it. We'll be safe there. When he gets back, he will discuss with you what happens next."

My father after all these years. "It's going to be so unreal to see him."

"I'm sure he feels the same way." Simon yawned. "We better get some sleep."

"Okay," Cammie said.

"Goodnight." Simon reached for the lamp.

She quickly slipped off her jeans and climbed under the covers. She heard Simon sigh when he rolled over. Closing her eyes, she hoped when she woke up her father would still be alive.

Chapter Four

Cammie stood over Simon sprawled out on his bed. "Simon?" He didn't move. "Wake up," she said louder.

"What's wrong?" he asked alert, one hand on his gun.

She walked in place. "I need to go running. I usually go every morning, but haven't since the abduction. My legs are cramping up."

Simon rubbed his eyes. "What time is it?"

"It's 5:00 a.m.," she said, wide-awake.

"Okay, I'm getting up." He pulled his shirt back over his head, giving her one last view of his awesomeness.

Cammie, already dressed, was anxious to do something normal again. She raised her arms above her head. "We need to stretch before we start running."

Simon stretched his arms above his head.

"Now just try to keep up," she said, grabbing the motel key and looking back.

"Cheater!" He shut the door and quickly caught up to her.

After a couple of miles, Simon turned to her, "We better head back."

"First one back to the motel gets all the hot water," Cammie told him, speeding up. She got there first, ran to the bathroom, and locked the door. Simon came in right behind her. She had a small suspicion he had let her win.

"Save me a little hot water," he called through the door.

"Maybe," she said in a singsong voice.

After they were both showered and dressed, Simon went to get them some breakfast from the gas station next door.

Five minutes later, he opened the door, holding up a bag and cardboard cup holder. "Hot tea and donuts."

"Did you get sugar?" She took the hot Styrofoam cup from him.

He reached into the bag and handed her few packets.

She smiled. "Thank you. How did you know?"

"At the drug store you got sweet tea. I like mine sweet, too." He stirred some sugar into his cup.

He was full of surprises. She had taken him for the type of guy that would drink something strong, like black coffee.

"Thanks for the run."

He nodded and handed her a glazed donut.

Great, first fast food now donuts. Good thing I talked him into a run. When they finished eating, they packed their clothes and Simon turned in the motel key.

"Are you ready to go get the ruby?" he asked.

She let out a nervous breath. "As ready as I'm going to be."

They got into the Corvette, Cammie's stomach in knots.

Simon looked over at her. "It's about an hour away from here."

"Are you coming into the bank with me?" she asked.

"No. You need to go alone," he said.

She was putting a lot of trust into someone she barely knew. "You'll be in the car waiting?"

"Yes."

Should I be worried? Everything he said made sense, but this whole situation is just bizarre. She really had no choice, but to trust him. If her father were really alive, all this would be worth getting him back.

Simon pulled the car in front of the bank. Cammie got

out and walked up to the door. Holding the empty purse in her shaking hands, she felt as if she were the one stealing the ruby. Uneasy, she walked up to the bank manager's desk.

"Hello. May I help you?" The heavyset man in a dark blue suit looked up at her.

Cammie sat down in the chair in front of his desk. "Yes, I need to get into my safe deposit box."

"Sure, account number please?" Cammie told him the number she had memorized.

"Yes, here it is," he replied, as he typed the number into the computer. "According to my records you are the correct age to obtain the contents of your box. This is a high security box, so I will need to scan your fingerprint print, Miss. Adams.

"Of course," she replied, coolly. *Almost there.*

He scanned her finger, nodded and stood up. "Right this way."

She followed him as he walked down the hall. He left her in a private room to examine the contents of her box. When she was alone, she unlocked the container and sat there for a moment to stare at it. *No turning back now.* She reached over and carefully opened the metal box. Inside was a black velvet box with a poem attached in her mother's handwriting. She took a deep breath and read it to herself.

Rubies deepest red, sapphires brilliant blue,
darling girl,
you are my true jewel through and through.

Her parents had really planned this out. She folded the poem in half and put it inside the empty purse. Hands shaking, Cammie carefully opened the black box and looked inside. The ruby was about the size of a large gumball. She picked up the ruby. *Wow!* It sparkled a deep crimson when she held it up to the light. The sheer beauty of the glassy, red gemstone consumed her for a few seconds. She put the ruby back inside the black box and dropped it into the vinyl purse. After she closed the empty metal safe deposit box, she called the bank manager back in.

"Everything in order?" he asked.

"Yes, I want to close my account here. I will no longer need this safe deposit box."

"Very well, I will just need your signature." He handed Cammie the proper paperwork.

*****

Simon tapped on the steering wheel as he waited for Cammie. He would have loved nothing better than to take that ruby himself, but he wasn't here for the ruby, he was here for Max. He had to stick to their plan and hoped Cammie didn't run into any trouble. He had told her it would go smoothly, but honestly, he didn't know. Even Max wasn't certain. Storing that ruby in the safe deposit box for twenty-two years hadn't been Max's idea, Cammie's mother had arranged it all.

Cammie was different than any woman he had ever known. *She's sweet, funny and innocent. She has a good heart. And damn why does she have to be so pretty?* This job was going to be harder than he originally thought.

When she walked out of the bank, he let out a sigh of relief.

*****

Cammie opened the door and got inside the Corvette.

"Did you get it?" he asked, as she sat down.

She nodded feeling nauseated. "Yeah, I got it."

Simon started the car. He drove a few blocks and pulled over. "Can I see it?"

Cammie got the box out of her purse and handed it to him.

He opened it and took out the ruby. Smiling, he studied the ruby, then whistled. "It's amazing. Good job." He handed it back to her.

She had half expected him to take it and run but guessed he was telling the truth after all. She'd keep the poem to herself. It didn't concern him anyway.

"How long until we reach my father?" she asked.

He pulled the Corvette back onto the road. "A couple hours."

She would see her father in a couple hours, something she had wanted for so long. *Why then, am I nervous?* "I can't believe he's alive."

He smiled. "Very alive and well."

She twirled her long hair and placed it over her right shoulder. "I don't even know what I'm going to say to him."

"I'm sure you'll think of something."

"Yeah like, nice to see you father, how's the weather, oh and by the way, thanks for lying to me my whole life." *How could they do this to me?*

Simon laughed. "Better late than never."

Cammie reached over and slapped his arm.

"Ow, what was that for?"

She shook her head. "For laughing at my life."

"Oh come on, lighten up. You are getting your father

back from the dead and you have the best bodyguard money can buy."

She rolled her eyes and looked out her window. *What will I even say to him? What will he say to me?* "I hope his place is nicer than that awful motel."

"Quite a bit. You're about to see."

They drove a while longer and passed some vineyards. Something was familiar. "Wait a minute. I've been in this area. He's lived this close to me all this time?"

"Just for the last four years. He lived in Canada before that."

Cammie shook her head. *Four years, he could have come to see me, but he didn't. An hour drive away and there I was.* She knew he was trying to keep them safe, although it hurt her that he didn't try harder to find a way.

Simon slowed down when they reached a row of mature trees. There was a tall, black iron fence surrounding the property. In the middle of the fence, was a break in the trees with a gate that opened to a long brick-paved driveway. *It looks like some kind of fortress.*

Simon slowly pulled the car up to the closed gate. A security camera was pointed at the car. When he typed a code in the metal box, the gate swung open and Simon drove the car through up a long winding driveway to massive house with an attached four-car garage. The limestone building looked like a miniature castle, complete with a turret. The house was so tall and beautiful.

"I'll let you two catch up," Simon said, as he opened her car door. He led her to the front door of the house. "See you later."

She watched Simon disappear into the garage. As she stood at the front door all alone, she felt faint. She rang the doorbell. Her father opened the door, even more handsome than she remembered. Tall, tan, dark-blonde hair and sparkling-blue eyes. He hadn't changed a bit, except for a few grays around his temples.

"Cammie, my darling girl, you're all grown up." He embraced her. Overwhelmed with emotion, she clutched him tightly, tears streaming down her face.

"Everything will be alright, Darling. I'm here now." He kissed the top of her head.

"I can't believe you are alive. I wanted to believe Simon, but I couldn't until I saw you for myself." She let go of him and stepped back. *It's really him.*

"We have so much to talk about. We have about thirty minutes, then I have a flight to catch. As soon as I return, I promise all your questions will be answered."

"Is mother really –"

Her father gently smiled and wiped her tears with his thumb as he did when she was a little girl. "Yes, she's in a better place. I'm sure she is looking down on us now, happy to see us reunited."

Cammie nodded her head. "So much has happened."

"Are you happy, Darling?"

Happy? A word I'd never use to describe my life. "It's been hard without you."

"I'm so sorry. I should have been there for you. You have every right to be angry with me," he said.

"I'm hurt and a little angry, but I never stopped loving you. Miles, a friend, tried to help me work through my loss. I also have Nora, my housekeeper, who is a dear friend and Dinah, my best girlfriend. They have all been there for me."

"I'm relieved to hear you weren't alone." Her father walked her over to the brown, leather sectional.

They sat down.

He placed a hand over hers. "Did Simon take good care of you?"

"Yes, but was it really necessary to hire him as my bodyguard?"

"I know you don't understand, but it was and I'm sorry. Your mother and I should have never put you in this situation."

You think? "No you shouldn't have. I thought I would be a lot angrier with you when I saw you, but someone once told me we can't change who we are and how we got here."

"That is wise. However, they forgot to add that we *can* change who we become. And I want to become an ordinary father."

Cammie smiled. "Father, you could never be ordinary, but I'm glad you want to try."

"Your mother and I only wanted the best for you. I truly am sorry."

She opened the purse and handed her father the poem.

"This is a surprise. I didn't know she wrote this. She used to sing this to you when you were little."

Cammie frowned. "Really? I don't remember."

"She stopped when you got older. We wanted to hide that part of our past from you, until the time was right."

"I guess the time wasn't right when I was fifteen," she said, quietly.

"We wanted to wait until you were an adult. We wanted you to become your own person first. We didn't want to influence the choices you would make."

"You have to stop protecting me. I need the truth from

you from now on. I can handle it and I expect it."

"Fair enough." He studied her face. "You are just beautiful. You look a lot like your mother did at that age."

Cammie tucked her hair behind her ears. "Do you miss her?"

"Always, but I have made peace with what happened." Her father stood up. "Darling, I have to go. I promise I will see you soon."

She took the black, velvet box out of her bag and handed it to her father. "This was supposed to be yours," he said, slowly taking it from her.

Cammie shook her head. "It's never been mine and I don't want it to be."

He hugged her tight and kissed her forehead. "Simon will stay with you until I get back. Be nice to him. He's been a loyal friend."

Cammie nodded and watched her father go out to the garage. She knew in her heart that he would come back safe. Fate would not dare take him from her twice.

Simon walked up behind her. "Everything's going according to plan. This will all be over soon. Then you'll be rid of me."

Cammie turned to him. "You're not so bad."

His hazel eyes shimmered with mischief. "Lots of people would argue that."

She looked around. The décor was old-world style. Lots of rich colors and textures, fit for a home that resembled a castle.

"Now we wait. Would you like a tour of your father's home?"

"He really owns this place?" she asked.

"Your father's very wealthy."

"So is this your home, also?"

"You could say that."

There were three floors. Simon walked her through the huge home. Everything was plush and luxurious.

"Here's your room." Gorgeous colorful paintings adorned the black and white damask papered walls, which reminded her of her mother's painting. She gasped when she saw the portrait of her family hanging over the white marble fireplace. The black, wood four-poster bed looked extremely comfy, especially after that cheap mattress at the motel.

Cammie could feel Simon watching her as she walked around the room.

"Your father has been working on this room for you for the last few months. He wanted you to feel at home."

Not sure how I feel about that. "So my room is on the same floor as yours?"

"Yeah, your father thought I should be close."

Hmm. Crossing paths with him in the middle of the night could pose a problem, especially if he went shirtless. She pushed that thought away and turned to him.

"It's absolutely beautiful. It reminds me of my old room growing up only this one is more sophisticated. That picture of my parents, I would've loved to have had that. The only pictures I had of them were inside this locket."

"That must've been hard. Well, it's yours. Your father found some old negatives and had it made for you."

"It's good to see her face." Cammie's eyes narrowed and her spine stiffened. "After the plane crash, our house caught fire. Were my parents responsible for that as well?"

"Yes. They didn't want anything to trace back to you.

Once you were safe with your aunt, they destroyed the house. Your father told me that was one of the hardest things he ever had to do."

"I loved that house." She paused. "My whole life has been a lie."

"Cheer up. Things will be okay now." He paused for a moment. "So what do you want to do?"

Cammie looked around. "How do you spend your time when you are not being a hero?"

"Sometimes, I watch movies. Want to watch one in the surround sound theater?"

"I don't know," she hesitated.

"You got something better to do?"

"I guess not. Maybe it'll help pass the time."

"I'll make the popcorn. You go find a seat."

Cammie went downstairs to the theater room. She opened the door and went inside and sat on one of three black-leather sofas on stadium like levels. She plopped her feet on the rectangular coffee table in front of the sofa. The walls were covered in dark fabric and the screen took up most of the front wall. *How many movies has my father watched in here while I thought he was dead?*

Simon came into the room carrying a large bowl of popcorn and two sodas on a teak tray. He sat down next to her, too close for her comfort.

"There are two other sofas," Cammie said, pointing to the other seats.

"But I have the popcorn." Simon winked and held out the bowl.

He has a point. "I guess if you put it that way." She grabbed a handful and paused before she stuffed it into her mouth. "Don't you have to start the movie?"

"Already taken care of, it's on a timer so it should be starting any minute." The lights started to dim and as Simon promised the movie came on the big screen. She munched on popcorn and watched an action-packed movie with mindless violence and impractical heroes. When Simon put his arm on the sofa behind her, she moved a few inches away from him. Heat rushed to her face when she felt his gaze on her a few times during the movie, but she acted like she didn't notice. She wished he didn't smell so good, it was distracting.

"Good movie," Cammie said, getting up, relieved it was over.

Simon stretched his arms over his head. "It was good, but I prefer the real life action."

She rolled her eyes. "Of course you do."

After they took their dishes to the sink, Cammie started washing them. When Simon reached for a clean bowl and dried it, he surprised her. *A tough guy, gun tucked in the small of his back, doing dishes. Who is this guy?*

Even though the house was huge, Cammie could feel the walls closing in around her. "I hate waiting. Are we stuck in this house or can we go someplace?"

Simon put away the last dish. "It's not safe until your father gets back. We have to stay on the property unless it's an emergency."

Cammie sighed and drained the dishwater. "That's not going to be easy."

"You think too much. Just stop thinking for once and live in the moment."

She shook her head. "You don't understand."

"Let's just try to make the most of being stuck here together. We could go for a swim. There's a nice pond in back."

"I don't have a swimsuit."

A wicked smile tugged at Simon's lips. "Neither do I, but it's getting dark and I promise not to look. When was the last time you did anything spontaneous?"

Her eyes widened and her mouth dropped open. "You mean go *skinny dipping*?"

"Are you chicken?" Simon headed to the back door.

"Of course not." She hated being called a chicken. "You stay on your side of the pond and I'll stay on mine." Cammie followed him down to the pond. She looked up at the moon. *Why do you have to be so bright tonight?*

Simon took off his shirt and started to take off his shorts.

She held up her hand. "Wait, turn around and let me go first."

Once she was sure he did what she'd asked, Cammie took off her clothes and jumped in. The cool, smooth water against her bare skin felt wonderful.

"Can I turn around now?"

"Yeah, this is great." She glided through the pond.

"No peeking," Simon teased, taking off his shorts. *Wow, he goes commando.* She turned her head away to hide her blush. The temptation to turn back was so strong she could hardly breathe.

Soon it was dark.

"I'm getting cold." She shivered. "Um, we don't have any towels."

Simon laughed. "How would that have been spontaneous if we would've stopped to get towels?"

She pointed to the house. "Bring me a towel, please."

"That would be the gentleman thing to do. Too bad I'm not a gentleman."

Cammie crossed her arms and frowned.

Simon swam up to her. He was so close she could feel his breath on her face. “Tell you what. If you promise not to mope around anymore, I’ll go get you a nice warm towel.”

She moved away from him. “Agreed, just hurry, I’m cold.”

Simon climbed out and water rolled off his tight butt. Suddenly she didn’t feel cold anymore as heat rushed through her body. He grabbed his clothes and ran into the house. *I just went skinny-dipping! What is wrong with me?* She felt guilty for having fun while her father was in danger and her friends back at home were probably worried.

A moment later, Simon strolled out of the house, fully dressed and carrying a huge towel as promised.

“Here you go.” He leaned over to put the towel on the dock.

“Thanks, I’ll meet you back inside.”

She waited until he got back to the house, then got out and dried off. Putting her clothes back on, she thought about everything that had happened since Greece. As she walked inside, she realized she was starting to see Simon differently.

“I’m going to bed. Do you need anything?” Simon asked.

“No, and Simon, thanks.”

“For what?”

His wet hair dripped down his shirt making it hard to concentrate. “For taking my mind off everything.”

Simon smiled. “You’re welcome.”

“Good night,” Cammie said, before going to her room.

*****

It had taken all his will power not to kiss Cammie. He'd had plenty of opportunity with the movie and then the pond. Simon didn't intend to get her naked, but his playboy instincts had kicked in before he could stop. The fire in her eyes when he'd called her chicken was unexpected.

Simon slipped off his clothes and got into bed. He tried to push Cammie out of his mind. *She's a job. No more, no less.* He would have to continue to remind himself of that fact. That and she was Max's daughter. Simon closed his eyes and recalled the look on Cammie's face when she saw the portrait of her parents. She loved her family that was evident. *What it would be like to love someone that much?*

Chapter Five

Cammie woke up in a strange, but comfortable bed. How surreal to wake up in her father's house, a father who she had thought to be dead just a few days ago. She took a quick shower and tried not to think about the men who took her, getting a hold of her father. After wiping the fogged mirror, she put on a little make-up. Once she was dressed in a pair of jeans and pink T-shirt she went downstairs to the kitchen fit for a gourmet chef. Simon stood over the stove making breakfast in blue jeans and a gray shirt.

"How do you like your eggs?" he asked.

She walked up behind him. "Fried. You cook?"

"Just breakfast. It comes in handy with women." He winked.

"I bet it does." She shook her head and poured them both some hot tea. Feeling odd, she sat down at the huge kitchen island made of sparkling, black granite.

Simon brought her the eggs and sat down next to her.

"Thanks." The bacon was just as she liked it, slightly chewy, like jerky. Her father's specialty, she hadn't had bacon like that since she was a kid. "Did my father teach you how to make bacon this way?"

"Nope, that's the way I've always made it. You like it?"

"Yes." She smiled and helped herself to another strip.

Simon took a drink from his stone mug. "You can make dinner."

Cammie wiped her mouth on a napkin. "I eat a lot of takeout. Don't really know how to cook."

"Oh. I think there are some frozen dinners in there. Maybe that would be safer." He stuck an entire strip of bacon in his mouth.

Cammie laughed. "Probably." She stood up and took her dishes to the sink.

"You surprised me last night."

She stopped to look at him. "Really, why?"

Simon got up and placed his dishes in the sudsy water and his hand grazed hers making her feel tingly.

A smirk tugged and his lips. "I didn't think you would actually get into the pond fully naked."

She bit her lip. "You called me chicken."

Simon stood close enough that she could smell the spice in his cologne. "Well, in that case, Cammie, you're too chicken to kiss me right now."

She stepped back a couple of inches. "Funny. I'm not going to kiss you no matter what you call me."

He grinned. "Why not?"

She ignored his question, but it would be nice to kiss him. *Not a good idea. This guy is my father's friend.*

When she didn't answer, he asked, "Want to play a game?"

She narrowed her eyes. "What kind of game?"

He got up and went to the hall closet. He looked inside, "We have Monopoly, cards or chess."

He'll never know what hit him. "Monopoly, I haven't played the game in years." She put the dishes away and went to the living room where he sat the game on the large square ottoman.

Simon took the game out of the box. "I'll get it set up."

"Do you cheat?" She watched him shuffle the yellow and orange cards.

"What's the matter, don't trust me?" He smirked.

Cammie pursed her lips. "No, I know what you used to do for a living, remember?"

Simon laughed. "What? You think I'm going to steal a

hotel off one of your properties?"

She pointed to her eyes and then to him. "I will be keeping a close eye, just in case."

"No cheating, I promise." He crossed his heart.

They played a long game of Monopoly, which ended when Cammie had hotels on most of the high priced properties causing Simon to go bankrupt.

"You can tell this is only a game. In real life, I would never go bankrupt," he said.

She laughed. "You're just mad that I beat you."

He hazel eyes lit up. "No, I don't mind. The look on your face when you took all my money was priceless."

Cammie stood up and stretched. Her legs were asleep from sitting too long. "Is it safe to go running?"

"Not outside the gates. We need to stay on your father's property."

Cammie frowned. "I need exercise."

A slight smile tugged at the corners of his mouth and he got a mischievous look in his hazel eyes.

"Swimming is not an option," she said, imagining what he was thinking.

His look turned serious. "How are you at jumping?"

Cammie raised an eyebrow. "Jumping?"

"I have a trampoline in the garage."

"What are you ten?" She laughed.

"Hey, don't knock it until you've tried it," he said.

"All right, let's go," she replied. *What will he do next?* For some reason, his spontaneity excited her. They walked out into the garage and she was surprised, yet again. The ceiling must've been twenty feet high and in the far corner was the promised trampoline. Simon smiled wickedly at her before he climbed onto the black circle and offered her a hand up.

She hopped a little until she started jumping. "This…is… so…fun!"

"Told you!"

"I might have to get one of these. This is really good exercise," she said, breathless. They bounced up and down and laughed like kids until Simon finally wore out and climbed down.

"Tired already?" she asked, still jumping.

He bent over with his hands on his thighs, out of breath. "You're in pretty good shape, I'll give you that."

Cammie smiled and nodded.

Simon disappeared into the house.

She continued jumping for a few more minutes. *I haven't laughed that much in a long time.* It felt good to laugh so much her sides hurt. Simon was a really fun guy to be around. He was so full of life and she could see why her father liked him.

*****

Hungry for dinner, Cammie opened the fully stocked freezer and pulled out two turkey dinners trying to ignore the sodium content that would undo the exercise she had done earlier. She plopped the plastic trays into the microwave and pushed start. She examined her nails as the oven nuked their food. *He better not get used to me cooking for him.* She grabbed some potholders off the counter and lifted out the steaming food.

"Dinner's ready," she called to him down the hall.

Simon walked in. "Should I be afraid? What is it?"

"Sliced turkey with gravy, mashed potatoes and green beans in a mushroom sauce and I'm not quite sure what this thing is, but I think it was supposed to be a brownie," she said, poking the hard lump with her fork.

"Sounds delicious. I know what will go perfect with dinner." He stood up and went to the wine fridge. After choosing a bottle of white wine and a couple glasses, he carried them to the table. They quietly ate their dinner.

Everything she had just gone through was overwhelming. First, she thought she was going to die. Then, she found out her father was alive and her mother had been murdered. And now, she was actually enjoying the company of her bodyguard a little *too* much. *How should I feel?* Too many emotions clouded her judgment.

"Are you still here, Cammie?" Simon interrupted her thoughts.

"Yes, just thinking about home."

"It won't be long and you'll be back where you belong."

Cammie smiled. Simon couldn't possibly understand what was going through her mind. She didn't understand it herself. She wanted to get back to get her new business going and to see Nora, Dinah, and Miles, but part of her would miss Simon. He made her feel like a carefree teenager. The one she had never had a chance to be. She had to grow up much too fast.

Simon stood up and tossed what was left of his dinner into the trashcan. "I'll be right back."

Cammie watched him walk out of the kitchen. The more time she spent with him the more attractive he got. *How is that even possible?* She threw away the remainder of her dinner, turned out the kitchen light and went into the living room.

He walked back into the room holding a box. "Your father told me you were quite the artist. We had some left over cans of paint and some brushes in the garage. I thought if you missed painting, you could paint something."

Her devastated art studio popped into her mind, but she quickly pushed it aside. Cammie looked inside the box at the five quarts of house paint and the one-inch trim paintbrushes. She lifted up a half-empty quart of satin Buttercream. She had to hold in a giggle. Not the typical paint an artist used, but maybe she could make it work. "Thank you, that's really thoughtful of you."

"Hey, I know it's not oil paint, but—"

Cammie took the box from him. "It's fine. Thank you." It was sweet. "I'll go paint something on the garage wall. It's a big white canvas just begging for color." She went out into the garage and sat down the box. Eyeing the wall before her, she shook the cans before taking out the flat screwdriver Simon had inside the box. Her inner eye mapped out an image as she mixed some of the colors together.

A couple hours later, Simon brought out a glass of ice tea for her. "Wow." His mouth dropped open at the small mural she'd painted of the pond out back. "It's amazing. You're really talented."

She laughed. "I've had lots and lots of practice." She took a long drink of the cold sweet tea.

Simon stood in front of the mural. "My favorite part is the moon's reflection on the pond."

Cammie threw the empty paint cans and used brushes in a trash bag.

"I better get washed up and go to bed." She opened the door.

Simon nodded. "Okay. Goodnight."

She walked up to him and gave him a quick kiss on the cheek. "Thanks for that." Before he could answer or respond she ran upstairs. She washed her hands and slipped on her T-shirt she'd been using for PJs, then got into bed. Feeling a bit happy, she pulled the fluffy white covers up to her neck.

*****

Cammie woke up and looked at the clock... 5 a.m. She was so used to waking up early to run her body was confused. She got dressed in the least dirty pair of jeans and T-shirt, one of the only three outfits she had here. Good thing her father had a washer and dryer. She couldn't put it off any longer. She would have to figure out those intimidating machines. They looked like some kind of spacecraft with all the buttons and lights and were even silver like a spaceship.

Cammie had never washed her own clothes. Nora took care of that task. Even when she lived in the hotel, the staff did her laundry. All she'd to do was bag up the dirty clothes and they would magically reappear in her suite clean. Before that, she was a kid and her mother did the laundry.

She gathered her dirty clothes and tiptoed down to the laundry room. She looked in the cabinets and found the laundry soap. *Okay, how does this work?* She pushed the button for a small load, then pushed the button for warm water. She heard the water come on and she tried to open the lid to put her clothes in, but it was locked. *No!* She tried to get the door open and stop the water. She bit her lip and started pushing buttons. The machine was not happy. All the buttons lit up at once which made loud spinning noises. *No! No! No!*

Simon came in behind her and laughed. "Having trouble, Sweetheart?"

Cammie blushed. "I've never had to use one of these. I think this washer is possessed."

Simon smiled, reached over to the machine and pushed a couple of buttons. The washer stopped what it was doing and the lid opened. He stepped back. "There you go. It helps if you put the clothes *into* the washer."

She rolled her eyes. "I was trying to." She put her clothes inside and then looked at the soap.

Simon reached out to show her where it went.

"No, I can figure it out." She peered inside the washer and saw a drawer for the soap. "See got it."

He laughed. "You can do mine next, if you want the practice."

"I don't plan on making this a habit." She stomped back to her room.

Simon gently knocked on the closed door.

She hated that she felt so embarrassed. "What?"

"I come in peace. You want to jump on the trampoline with me?"

Sit here and sulk or go get exercise with Mr. Hotness? No brainer. Cammie opened the door. "Fine."

They went to the garage and climbed onto the trampoline.

"Sorry I laughed at you. You've really never washed clothes?" he asked.

"I know it's crazy, but no. In my defense, I haven't ever seen a washer and dryer like those."

"Yeah, they are state of the art and are actually really easy to use once you know how." Simon looked over at the mural she had painted. "I think your father will love it."

"I hope so." She smiled. "I do like jumping, but I miss running. I think I've already gained a couple pounds."

"Well, I think you look great."

"Thanks."

He jumped circles around her. "From. Every. Angle."

She slapped his arm and got down.

"What? I'm a guy, I notice these things."

Cammie went to her room to take a shower. She couldn't believe some of things that came out of Simon's mouth. The bad thing was, she was thinking the same things about him, but she wouldn't dare say them. Until now, she'd never really felt a strong attraction for someone. It was a strange feeling. Someone that actually enjoyed making fun of her quite often, Simon was almost the complete opposite of Miles.

After they ate breakfast, Simon asked her if she wanted to see something amazing.

"What kind of something?" she asked, suspicious.

"My diamond collection, it means a lot to me. Would you like to see it?"

Curiosity got the best of her. "Okay."

She followed him to his room. He walked over to the fireplace where a turquoise lion statue sat like a regal sentry. Simon pushed down on the lion's head. The fireplace moved and a small room was revealed.

Cammie's eyes widened. "A secret room?"

"Yeah, even better than a safe." He winked.

It was like a small jewelry store only about the size of a walk-in closet, but the back wall was lined with a glass case. Colorful diamonds scattered over black velvet. The diamonds were tiny compared to the ruby, but there were dozens of them.

She walked around slowly to examine the sparkle. They were beautiful. It looked as if a fairy had sprinkled large, multi-colored fairy dust. Gray, blue, purple, pink, brown, orange, yellow and green diamonds. In the center, her eyes were drawn to a gorgeous, white gold necklace with round cut diamonds and a gold medallion hanging from the center. For a split second, she could see why her parents loved jewels and why Simon had *collected* these.

Amazing. "Are all these diamonds?"

He winked. "Every last one."

"I never knew diamonds came in all these colors."

"They're rare, but yes, the colors are natural. There's only one color I never acquired, the rarest of all the diamonds...red."

"How much are all these worth?" she blurted out. "Never mind. Don't tell me. It's better if I don't know." Cammie walked up and down looking at all the vibrant colors, a rainbow of diamonds. All the diamonds were loose, except for the necklace.

He eyed her. "Would you like to try it on?"

She shook her head. "Do you ever feel bad about taking these?"

"No, I've only taken them from people who didn't deserve them. Drug lords, criminals, that sort. I get great satisfaction from taking these precious babies off their hands."

"That sounds really dangerous. Is that who my parents took the ruby from, someone bad?"

His lip twitched. "That's not my story to tell."

"This all seems so unreal."

"In a jewel thief's world, it's very real." Simon scooped up a handful of the colorful jewels. "Hold out your hand."

Cammie did as he asked and he sprinkled them into her cupped hand.

She looked down at the diamonds in her palm. "I've

never seen such natural beauty."

Simon took a lock of her hair and tucked it behind her ear. "I hadn't either until I met you, Sweetheart."

She blushed. "I don't even come close to these." She gently rolled the diamonds around in her hand to watch the light bounce off of them.

"Oh, but you do and don't even realize it."

She handed the jewels back to him. The little room was getting hot. *Time to bail.*

"Thanks for showing me." She glanced at the necklace one more time, before walking out.

Simon closed the fireplace wall and the jewel room disappeared as if it never existed.

Cammie hurried out of his room down to the kitchen where it was safer.

Simon followed behind her. He walked into the kitchen. "How about a glass of wine?" he asked, already pouring.

Cammie nodded. They sat on the sectional and watched the sunset through the large window. The wine made her feel warm and tingly. Or maybe that was Simon.

Simon's eyes met hers. "So are you involved with anyone?"

"It's complicated." She emptied her glass of wine.

Simon immediately refilled it. "What's that mean?"

Maybe it would help to talk about it, besides wine always loosened her lips. "We met at his hotel when I was fifteen. I thought my parents were dead. I was all alone."

The house grew dark. Simon reached over and turned on a lamp.

"Miles took me under his wing. He tried to fix me I guess. He fell in love, I didn't."

Simon ran a finger along her cheek sending some kind of electric sensation through her. "So you were broken?"

Cammie ran her finger along the rim of the glass. "Yeah. He was my best friend and my only family. He was determined to marry me. We're still great friends, but that's all." She could feel her eyes misting up, but feeling talkative, she went on. "Besides it would never work with Miles, he wants children."

"So you didn't want to have a child, why?" Simon started to fill her glass again, but she held up her hand. He sat the bottle back down on the end table.

"I don't know. I just don't." *Children are terrifying.*

He put his hand over hers. "Miles sounds important to you."

She moved her hand away from his. "I love Miles. I always will, but not the way he needs me to. I don't want to hurt him and I don't want to lose his friendship." She swallowed to choke back a cry. It would be so easy to just slip into Simon's strong arms and let him comfort her. Instead, she stood up. "It's getting late."

He smiled. "It's not so late."

"I'll see you in the morning." She didn't trust herself to be alone with him after having two glasses of wine and feeling vulnerable.

*****

Simon watched Cammie go up to her room. *Shit, what am I doing?* He rubbed his face. *Why does she have to be so pretty and sincere? I want her, damn it.* He wanted her as bad as he'd ever wanted any diamond, maybe more. He couldn't betray Max. Time for a very cold shower. He shook his head as he made his way upstairs to his room, which was dangerously too close to hers.

Chapter Six

Cammie opened her eyes and looked around when she heard a knock.

"Are you awake? I just got word from your father," Simon called, through the door.

She sat up in bed. "Yes. Give me a second." Tired, she got up and slipped into a pair of jeans and lime green T-shirt. When she opened the door, she found Simon waiting in the hall.

"Your father ran into a little trouble, but nothing he couldn't handle. He's hoping he can get back in a couple days." Simon stood leaning against the wall with his arms crossed.

Cammie bit her lip. "You are sure he's all right?"

"Absolutely sure, don't worry."

Something made her want to confide in this man. "Simon, I want to show you something."

"Okay." He followed her into her room. She went over to a huge, white bookcase and pulled out a leather-bound book. She opened the book and removed the folded poem from her mother and the leaf and handed them both to him.

"This was with the ruby in the safe deposit box."

He read the poem her mother had written. "It sounds like after you were born, you became so much more valuable to her than any jewel ever could. You were her new treasure." He handed the paper back to her.

"My father said she used to sing it to me when I was a baby."

"That sounds nice," he said. "And this olive tree leaf?"

So that's what it is. "Olive tree? I wasn't sure what type of tree it was from."

"Why do you have it?"

"Before I was abducted, someone was in my bedroom late at night. I thought I was seeing things or dreaming. I know it was stupid, but there aren't normally break-ins in my community. The next morning my mother's painting was gone. It was the only painting I had of hers. The painting was of me as a baby, wearing a pearl necklace, sitting with her jewelry box."

"The painting itself wasn't what they were after. Was her signature on the front?"

Cammie nodded. "Yes."

"The men who were after the ruby were looking for anything that might lead them to it. They must've seen her signature on the painting. So what does that have to do with this?" He held up the leaf.

Cammie stuck her hands in her pockets. "Well, I was very upset that the painting was stolen. I looked for clues and found this in my art studio."

Simon's eyes widened. "You looked for clues? After you were just robbed? Are you crazy?" He shook his head.

She crossed her arms. "The painting means a lot to me. I want it back."

"Let me get this straight. You'll give away a ruby worth more than you can imagine, but you'd risk your life to hunt down a valueless painting?"

"Exactly. The ruby means nothing to me. My mother's painting is priceless."

Simon smiled. "I'll help you get it back. If you do something for me."

Uh oh. "What?"

"Have a picnic with me."

She smirked. "A picnic?"

"Yep, I've always wanted to have one."

Cammie drew her eyebrows together. "You've never been on a picnic?"

"No. You want me to help you or not?"

"Yes." *Who is this guy? How could someone have never have been on a picnic?*

He went into the kitchen, opened up the stocked pantry door and removed one of the cookbooks. "We can pick out something and make it together. Then we can pack up our meal, take it out by the pond and eat on the dock."

"I guess we could try," she replied, taking the cookbook and flipping through the pages. "What about chicken salad? Is there any chicken in the freezer?"

Simon shook his head. "No, but I think we have some in a can." He looked through the cans on the bottom three shelves. "Here, canned chicken." He handed her the small can.

"That'll work. I wouldn't know what to do with a raw chicken anyway."

Simon laughed.

She skimmed the chicken salad recipes. "What about walnuts?"

Simon went into the panty and came out with a small can of mixed nuts. "We can dig the walnuts out."

She smiled and nodded taking the nuts from him.

"I saw some mayo and the other ingredients so I think we can make chicken salad. What else should we have?"

Simon took the cookbook from her and scanned through the pages. "Chocolate chip cookies."

"Sure, every picnic needs cookies." They made chicken salad and dessert. When they finished the house smelled like warm chocolate chip cookies. They placed the food and a jug of sweet iced tea in a paper grocery bag. Simon got a big throw blanket and they headed outside for the pond.

The sun had warmed the wood of the dock. Simon spread out the blanket and Cammie started unpacking the food. She took two plastic cups and poured them some sweet tea. *Kind of bizarre, but nice.*

"Hey, this is pretty good," Simon said, with a mouth full of chicken salad.

"So we can cook, after all."

He smiled. "Who knew?"

Cammie chewed as she looked at Simon lounging on the blanket. He was wearing a thin green V-neck sweater revealing part of his smooth chest. His dark blue jeans were just tight enough to make her think back to their evening skinny-dipping. She blushed and quickly looked away.

"I have that effect on women," he said, embarrassing her even more.

Cammie played it off like she had no idea what he was talking about. "What?"

"Your cheeks look a little flushed."

Cammie shrugged. "It must be the sun. I haven't got on any sunscreen."

Simon took a bite of a warm gooey cookie. "We make a good team," he said, pointing to the cookies.

"Yeah, it was fun. Maybe I should start cooking."

Once they finished eating, Cammie started packing up the dishes and Simon folded up the blanket.

"So you'll help me get my mother's painting back?"

"It could be dangerous. I'll have to check with Max first."

Cammie crossed her arms. "I'm getting that painting

back with or without your help."

Simon smiled. "I like your spirit, Sweetheart. You've got guts."

"So how do we get it?"

"*We* don't. I'll get with your father to see if he can manage getting a hold of it. If not, I'll see what I can do when he gets back." Simon pointed to a small boat at the edge of the dock. "Do you want to go on a boat ride?"

She looked around. *What else do I have to do?* "Why not?"

Simon helped her into the little boat. He started the motor and they slowly whirled around the little pond. The cattails swayed in the warm breeze.

"Do you think you'll ever look for the red diamond?" she asked.

"I kind of gave up the jewel business, but it would be nice to complete my collection someday. Why?"

"Just wondering."

They both jumped when Simon's cell phone rang. He answered and Cammie listened to the one sided conversation.

"How many of them...They must have put a tracker on you after I got Cammie away...Are you wearing anything from that day...Okay, take off your shoes, leave them in the kitchen...Can you get to the secret room I told you about...The phone won't work once you go in...Stay put until we can get there." He hung up the phone, took one look at Cammie and stopped her. "I'll explain on the way. We have to go now." They got out of the boat and ran to the house. He packed some extra guns and they got in the car. Simon had a ruthless look in his eyes that worried her.

Cammie felt clammy and sick. "Was that Eve?"

"Yes. She was sitting in the living room looking out the window. She saw a van pull up in the driveway. She grabbed the emergency phone I left her and called me. When she looked outside again she saw three of the guys that had abducted her getting out of the van. She doesn't think they saw her," Simon explained, in a rush.

"We have to get there in time what if –"

"She's safe. She'll be okay until we get there." He looked over at her. "They must have put a tracker inside her shoe. I had her take off the shoes so they would think that we were on to them and just left the shoes there. I told her about a secret room to hide in, just like the one I showed you last night, only empty."

"What if they find where she's hiding?" Cammie trembled.

"They won't. I've used that room before. It's so well designed even an engineer would have trouble finding it."

"Do you think when they find the tracker they'll just go away?" Cammie asked, hopeful.

"Maybe, but more likely they'll be there waiting making sure she doesn't come back." Simon was driving so fast Cammie felt sick. She didn't dare slow him down though, every minute counted.

"Do you have a plan in case they are still there?"

"My plan, Sweetheart, is to get us all out alive." He winked.

Cammie cringed. "Not a good time for jokes."

"It'll be okay. You'll see. Do you know how to shoot a gun?" Simon asked.

"Telling me it will be okay, then asking if I can shoot is not reassuring me," she said, through clenched teeth. "And the answer is no, I don't."

"Point, aim, and squeeze the trigger. Aim for the chest. It's the biggest target. As a precaution, I want you to have this," he said, handing her a small gun.

Cammie took the gun from him like it was a grenade about to go off. Stun guns were one thing, guns with bullets another.

Simon looked at her and shook his head. "You have to squeeze the trigger for it to shoot."

"You're the bodyguard, why do I have to have a gun?" She looked at it on her lap with the barrel pointed away from her.

"It's only a precaution. There are only so many times I can rescue you and Eve." The familiar burn of tears came by surprise when Simon reached over and took her hand. It felt strong and she couldn't pull away.

"Hey, have I let you down yet?" He gently squeezed her hand. "I promise we will all get out of this unhurt. Trust me." Somehow, his touch calmed her. It was as if some of his confidence was transferring to her. She felt braver.

"We're almost there. I'm going to park the car about a half a mile from the farmhouse. There's an old barn we can hide the car in. I want you to stay right behind me. Hold on to the gun, but please don't shoot me." He looked at her like he was only half joking and she nodded. "I'm going to sneak in the house from the back. There are lots of trees to hide in. Just do what I tell you."

They walked quietly through the dark woods. Simon was two feet in front of her with his gun drawn.

Cammie had both hands on her gun and felt like she was in a movie. When they got close enough to the house to see the van, Cammie let out a whimper.

"They're still here. That's good and bad. Good because if they are still here, they haven't found your aunt. Bad because, I have to go in and get her out."

Cammie's adrenaline kicked in. "Go get her. I'll be your lookout like in Greece. Only this time, I won't be able to talk to you so I'll just shoot at anyone of them who comes toward me."

He looked at her surprised. "Okay. You stay hidden here. Be careful, your father will kill me if anything happens to you. Remember, point, aim, squeeze."

Cammie nodded and watched Simon sneak to the back of the farmhouse. She stood there in shock realizing she was all alone in the dark. Her grip tightened on the gun. She didn't hear anything except the sound of an owl hooting in the distance. About twenty minutes passed and she saw shadows of the three men walk outside and get into the van. The van drove off and she let out a sigh of relief. No gunshots were fired. The thugs left and everyone was still alive. *Thank God.* Simon and Eve came out of the house and ran toward her. Eve had a bag with her.

"Just as I was slipping in the back window, one of them got a call and told the others that they would come back tomorrow. I didn't even have to do anything except get Eve out," Simon said, almost disappointed. "We're going to get out of here, but there's something I have to do first. Wait here." He ran back up to the house and went into the garage. He started pouring gasoline all around the house and lit it on fire. He ran back to them. "Now when they come back, there'll be nothing left to lead them to us. Let's go." The three of them ran down to where the car was hidden and squeezed into the Corvette.

Cammie hugged Eve. "Are you okay?"

Eve nodded. "I am now. Thank goodness for that secret

room or who knows what would've happened."

Simon looked over at them. "Sorry about that. I thought you were out of danger. I won't make that mistake again. Until Max returns, you'll have to stay with us."

"Fine with me, at least I got to grab my clothes before you burned the house down to the ground."

"It should only be a few more days and my father will be back and all this will be over," Cammie said.

"I'm so exhausted. I really just need to sleep. I've tried, but I haven't really slept much since all this has happened."

Simon glanced at Eve. Cammie saw the concern on his face and looked at her aunt noticing the dark circles under her eyes. "If you really want to get some restful sleep, I have some sleeping pills back at home that will knock you out for a couple of days."

Eve nodded. "I think I'll try that. I literally have only had a few hours of sleep a night."

"You'll be able to get some sleep now. My father's estate is secure and Simon will protect us." Cammie was sorry that her aunt had to be involved in all this. It was taking its toll on her. She should have insisted her aunt come with them from the beginning. If she wouldn't have had Simon, she'd probably look just as bad as her aunt.

*****

Simon took a drink of his tea and glanced down the hall toward Cammie as she took her aunt to her room. Maybe it was a good thing that happened, with Eve here now he'd have to behave himself. Why did everything about Cammie concern him so much? Like the fact she didn't even know how to use a gun. *How will she protect herself once I'm no longer her bodyguard?*

*****

Eve was still lying on her side, covers pulled up to her neck. Cammie walked up to her and brushed the blonde curls out of her face to make sure she was still breathing. When she was sure that her aunt was okay, she closed the door and walked down the hall.

"Is she still out?" Simon asked.

"Yes, those pills you gave her last night are really helping. She looks like she's resting peacefully. She hasn't even moved. I had to check to make sure she was breathing."

"Yeah, they are strong, but perfectly safe. Your father used to take them when he couldn't sleep. He would be out for a long time, too."

Cammie bit her lip. "My father had trouble sleeping?"

"Yes, he worried about you a lot."

"There were a handful of times I've had trouble sleeping. There were times I would wake up in the night and think someone was in my room. Come to find out someone was." She shivered, just thinking about it.

Simon's face got serious. "All I can say is they're lucky they didn't hurt you."

"What would my father have done?"

"Not just your father." He searched her eyes. "I think if anyone ever hurt you, I'd kill them."

Cammie stiffened. "Don't kill anyone for me, I'm just a job."

Simon shook his head. "You mean more to me than a job, now."

"I do?" *Why does that make me happy?*

"I know you're my best friend's daughter and you have some weird complicated thing with Miles, but somehow you make me want you more than I ever wanted any jewels. Maybe all this happened for a reason."

Cammie took a deep breath. She couldn't believe what he just said. "I feel something for you too and it scares me. I'm confused." *Maybe if he didn't smell so damn good.*

Simon stepped closer to her. "I have an idea."

"What?" she whispered.

"Let me kiss you. If you feel nothing, then I'll forget about you." Cammie didn't know what to say. She wanted his lips on hers so bad it hurt, but it was bad timing.

"I can't."

For the first time Simon's cocky smile was replaced with a disappointed frown.

"I can't, because if I let you kiss me, I may not be able to control what happens next." She got up from the sofa and walked outside.

Simon sighed and got up to follow her out to the pond. They both sat on the dock.

"You can't just drop a bomb on me like that and walk off." His smile was back and he looked hotter than ever.

"What happens after, Simon?"

"I don't know, but I want to find out." He reached over and took her head in his hands. He gently brushed his lips over hers. When she didn't pull away, he kissed her more heatedly. Cammie let him kiss her and she kissed him back with more passion than she even knew she had.

He put his strong arms around her and laid her down on

the dock. She loved and hated how good he felt against her, but the timing was all wrong. Simon slipped off her shirt and took off his. She ran her fingers down his ripped stomach. Just as she was about to give in to her desire, something pulled her away. While she wasn't a virgin, Miles was the only man she'd ever been with. She was sure Simon was used to more experienced women.

"I can't, not like this. My father is out there in a dangerous situation risking his life. I can't do this right now."

Simon sat up and handed her shirt back to her. He sighed. "I know. But what does this mean? Where does that leave us?"

Cammie looked at him. "There isn't an *us.*"

"There almost was." He winked and sighed. "I don't think I can just let you go."

"You're a great guy, Simon Fisher. You'll be fine without me." *Why am I fighting this so bad when what I really want, is for him to make me feel passion and love the way I thought I never would?*

"Your father would probably kill me anyway." He turned away from her, hiding his emotions.

"Yes, most definitely." *Too late, he already pulled back.* "Let's go inside, make a snack and talk. I want to hear about your time with my father." She stood up.

He followed her back into the house and into the kitchen. "Okay, but if I tell you stories you have to tell me more about you."

Cammie nodded. "Deal."

"I'll make the popcorn and you can check on your aunt. Give her a couple more of these and she'll be back to herself tomorrow." He handed her two pills.

*****

Cammie sat cross-legged and faced Simon who was stretched out with his legs propped up on the large ottoman in front of them. A big bowl of hot buttery popcorn sat between them.

"What do you miss about stealing jewels?" Cammie asked.

"The rush."

"Did my father ever talk about me?"

"Yes, all the time. He wondered what you looked like, what you were doing, if you were happy."

Cammie sighed and took a sip of her sweet tea. "At first, I wasn't sure I would forgive him. But he is my father and I'll always be his little princess. I'm just sad he missed so much of my life."

"You two will have plenty of time to catch up."

Cammie's eyes narrowed. "I know, but has he changed, really?"

"Yes, I can say for sure, he has put that lifestyle behind him. Go easy on him. He's been through a lot."

She took a handful of popcorn. "I'll try. So what about you? Where do you go from here?"

"I haven't thought about it." He paused. "Okay, it's my turn to ask the questions. What is the best memory you have of your parents?"

"That's easy. When I was seven, I woke up from a terrible nightmare and ran into my parents' room crying. My father told me I had to be brave and chase the nightmare away. He said I had to make the nightmare afraid of *me*. My mother played along. They got me dressed for battle with things around the house. I had a lampshade on my head and a broom for a sword.

"They marched me right back into my room and told me to shout for nightmare to never come back. I must have looked so silly standing there waving my broom screaming at the top of my lungs to an empty room. But my parents never cracked a smile. They just stood by me until I was confident enough to get back into bed and go to sleep."

Simon laughed. "And did you have any more nightmares?"

Cammie shook her head. "Not for a long time. I look back now and appreciate how unconventionally they solved all my childhood problems." In all the years she had known Miles, he never had asked her what the best memory of her parents was. In fact, she had never shared that memory with anyone until now. She and Simon connected in a way she had never connected with anyone. *What does that mean?*

"So, tell me about the best adventure you've ever been on," Cammie said.

"You mean besides this one?"

"Not counting this one." She smiled.

"When I found some abandoned huts in South Africa. I actually lived in one for a few weeks. I acquired some of my rarest diamonds there."

"I can't imagine what that would be like. I don't think I could ever do that," she said.

"You don't give yourself enough credit. You're one of the toughest women I've ever known." He winked.

She blushed. "It's getting late. I should get some sleep."

"Would you like to sleep in my room tonight?"

Cammie sighed. "I can't."

He shrugged. "Can't blame me for trying."

She sighed. "Goodnight."

"Goodnight." Simon kissed her quickly before she stood up.

Taken by surprise, Cammie briefly kissed him back, before pulling away.

"Simon, I –" Was all she could say, then she walked to her room and shut the door. She got undressed and got into bed, then spent the next thirty minutes convincing herself not go down the hall to Simon's bed.

*****

Simon woke up when he heard a noise downstairs. He grabbed his gun and pointed it toward the stairway. When Max walked by the stairs, Simon let his shoulders relax and put his gun away. He hurried downstairs to greet his friend.

"It's over. The ruby is back in the hands of the rightful owner."

Simon patted his back. "I knew we could do it. Now you can have your daughter back in your life."

Max nodded. "How is she?"

That is the question. "I think she's ready to get back to go home."

Max looked toward the stairway. "Is she still asleep?"

"Yeah, Eve's upstairs in the guest room. She's fine, too."

Max gave Simon a bear hug. "Thank you so much my friend. I couldn't have done this without you."

"You're welcome. Hey look, I need a distraction for a while. I'm going to head south."

Max nodded. "South? Is everything okay?"

Simon shoved his hands in his pockets so Max wouldn't see them shaking. "Yeah, you know I hate goodbyes.

Could you just tell Cammie I had to go, but I'll never forget the pond?"

Max's eyebrows shot up.

"I have my bags in the Corvette. I'll see you soon." Simon left before he had to explain.

*****

Cammie woke up still feeling tired. She had tossed and turned all night. Maybe she should let Simon in. Maybe he would be right for her. Maybe two people who weren't perfect could be perfect for each other. She ran her fingers through her messy hair, then walked out of her room and bounced down the stairs to see Simon.

Her father sat at the kitchen island with a mug in his hand. "It's time to get your life back, Darling." He set down the steaming drink.

"You're back! Is it over?" Cammie hugged him and smiled.

He sighed. "Yes, finally."

"The ruby's back where it belongs?"

"Yes."

She hated to ask, but had to know. "Was anyone killed?"

Her father held onto her shoulders. "No."

Cammie let out a breath she didn't even realize she had been holding. She could live with her father being an ex-jewel thief, but didn't think she could handle it if he were a murderer. "Good. Eve's here, have you spoken with her?"

Her father stood up. "Not yet, I thought we'd work things out when you got back home. I have a lot of explaining and apologizing to do."

"I hope she'll forgive you. I can't stand the thought of my only two family members not getting along. I just got you both back and Christmas is only a few weeks away."

"It'll work itself out. Now you just need to get back home and get back to your life."

"Okay. You're staying here, right? You won't leave me again?"

"Of course not, Darling."

Cammie hugged her father. "I'm happy you're alive."

"I'm sorry that you had to be alone for so long."

She didn't want him to feel guilty. "I always had my friends."

"Go get ready and I'll get you back home safe and sound." Cammie took a shower and dried her hair. She was so excited to see her father she realized she didn't get the chance to talk to Simon, yet.

"Where's Simon?" she asked, her father when she came back downstairs.

"He wanted me to tell you he couldn't stand goodbyes. He said something like, remember the pond." He raised his eyebrows.

Cammie nodded and ignored her father's questioning gaze. *He's gone.* She wasn't sure if she was okay with him leaving. *Damn.* Maybe she was just another quest to him. She took a deep breath. "I'm ready to go home."

*****

Cammie called Nora and asked her to meet her, since she didn't have a key to her house. When her father pulled out of the driveway, she felt torn. *He wouldn't disappear again, would he?* He waved, so she smiled and rang the doorbell. When Nora opened the door, her father drove away.

"You're home! I was worried, Dear."

Cammie hugged her. "I have some wonderful news."

"I'll put some tea on," Nora said, walking toward the kitchen. Cammie followed her. Nora got the tea brewing in the tea maker then turned to her.

Cammie patted the other dining chair. "Come sit."

Nora sat down beside her.

"I had some serious family issues to address. I recently found out my father is alive." *Among other things.*

"Really? That's wonderful news." Nora patted her hand. "He didn't die in the plane crash?"

"No. It's a complicated story that doesn't really even matter."

"Of course not. The important thing is that you have him back."

"I also made amends with my Aunt Eve. I don't know if I ever told you, but I have an aunt that I had not spoken to in a really long time. She is my mother's only sister. I want you to meet them both, soon. You'll love them."

"I am sure I will." Nora paused. "Dear, I do not want to pry. Maybe I should not say anything, but I think of you as family and I feel you should know. While you were away, Miles was a mess. He was acting out of sorts. I think he really missed you."

She frowned. "Did he say something to you?"

"Not really. Just that you left without saying goodbye and he was worried."

Cammie bit her lip. "Thanks for telling me."

"If you ever need to talk, I am always here for you." She patted her hand again and smiled. Nora didn't pry about all the details of her absence. Good thing since she couldn't tell her or anyone else the full truth.

Nora got up to pour them both some tea. Cammie was glad to have the company, but realized Nora could have been in the middle of something when she called her.

Cammie smiled. "Thank you. I may take a few weeks off. I need to do some thinking before I take my first case. With the holidays coming up, it'd probably be better to wait anyway."

"Okay. I am so happy that your father is alive." Nora hugged her.

"Well, thanks for letting me in the house. Will I see you tomorrow?"

"Of course. Laundry day."

*****

For a few seconds, Miles just stood there, then he embraced her. Cammie called him when Nora left and thirty minutes later he was on her doorstep.

She didn't realize he'd take her absence so hard. "I'm sorry I had to leave without explaining."

"Cammie, you need to tell me what is going on and why you left like that. Imagine my surprise when you just disappeared. Couldn't you have at least called me?"

"I couldn't tell you where I was going, because I didn't know I was going anywhere. I went for my usual morning run and about halfway through, I was abducted."

Miles' eyes widened. "Abducted –"

"Don't freak out, I'm okay." She motioned him to the sofa and they both sat down.

Miles nodded. "Okay, go on."

"I was abducted and taken to this warehouse. I was really scared. Anyway, I was drugged and when I woke up, I was in Greece. This guy saved me and told me he was a friend of my fathers, then he told me my father was alive and the man kidnapped me to get back at my father for some old grudge." Her story sounded concocted even in her own ears.

Miles looked at her like she was from another planet. "You were in Greece and your father is alive?"

She nodded, hardly believing it herself.

"What does this have to do with your aunt?"

She should have thought her story out better, before calling him. "It's complicated." Was all she could come up with.

"I was worried sick. In the seven years I've known you, you've never disappeared like that."

"I'm sorry. But hey look, I'm fine. I want you to meet my father and aunt soon." She flashed back to her and Simon laughing, jumping on the trampoline. She quickly pushed that thought out of her head as fast as it had popped in.

"You didn't say much about the guy who rescued you. He didn't hurt you, did he?"

"Simon is a very close friend of my father. He didn't hurt me, he would never hurt me."

He sighed and rubbed his temples. "You must be exhausted. Maybe I could stay and we could order dinner in."

Cammie bit her lip. "I need some time alone, okay?"

"Oh, okay. If that's what you want." He stood up, looking disappointed. "I'm glad you're back." He hugged her tight.

"I'll call you tomorrow," she said, walking him to the door. She looked around at her big empty house and felt the wetness on her face before she even heard her own sobs. Finally, at home alone, she knew she couldn't hold the emotions in any longer. She cried for many reasons. For Simon, she cried for what could have been. For her father, she cried happy tears of joy that he was alive. For her mother, who was murdered. She climbed into her sleigh bed and pulled her comforter around her.

Chapter Seven

Cammie dragged herself out of bed. She dropped her clothes to the bathroom floor and looked in the mirror. Her eyes were still red and puffy, though she had no tears left to fall. Hopefully, a hot shower would help her feel better. Sighing, she got into the tub and turned the water as hot as she could take it.

She stood under the water in a trance as steam filled the bathroom. Only when the stream turned cold, did she turn off the faucet. In a zombie-like state, she got dressed and dried her hair. She gazed at the mirror. Even though she looked like herself, she felt different.

Cammie walked out to her art studio. Nora must have cleaned the place up for her. It was almost as if nothing ever happened. She put a fresh canvas on the easel and dabbed some paint on her brush. As she stared at the blank canvas, all she could think about were brightly colored diamonds and a bodyguard named Simon.

She tried to force those thoughts out of her head and painted a sunset. She painted fiercely and it showed, not her best work. She had never thrown away a piece of art, but she tossed this one into the trash before the paint even had time to dry. She knew what she needed. She called Dinah to get some much needed advice.

"It's me. Is it a bad time?"

"Oh, hi, no it's fine. Joey's taking his nap. So how are you? Are you back?" Dinah asked.

"Yes, did Nora call you?"

"I called last week and Nora said you were away helping your aunt with something."

"So much has happened I don't know where to begin."

"Start from the beginning. Since when are you talking to your aunt?"

Cammie told her the same story as she had told Miles, in addition, more details about Simon.

"You should hear the way your voice lights up when you talk about Simon."

"I know. I don't know what to do. Surely, I haven't fallen in love with him," she said, trying to convince herself more than Dinah.

"You went through so much together. Plus, it doesn't hurt that he is your father's best friend, your favorite person in the world. Other than me, of course," she joked.

"I feel so confused."

"You need to try to sort out your feelings for Simon. Do you want to come over tomorrow? My babysitter is sick, but I would love to see you. We could just hang out here."

"Yes, I'd like that."

"How about noon? I'll make lunch."

"Sounds great."

"Try not to worry too much. Things will work out. See you tomorrow."

*****

Cammie sat across from Miles in The Kipton hotel dining room. He had sectioned off a private area for them in the corner. A plate of fresh fruit and croissants were in the middle of their small, round table.

"How did you sleep last night?" Miles asked.

"Good," she lied.

He poured her some hot tea.

She took a croissant and spread butter over it. "Thanks."

Miles looked at her. "Since when do you eat butter?"

Cammie looked down at her croissant she had just absent-mindedly buttered. "I don't know. It just tasted so plain." *Kind of like my life before Simon.*

Miles raised an eyebrow. "I have about an hour before my meeting. What did you want to talk about?"

She had to make things right with him. "I'm sorry for any pain I've caused you. It was never my intention to hurt you."

Miles put his hand over hers. "It's my own fault. I worry about you too much."

"You'll always be my friend, but that's all."

"So you keep telling me." He winked.

He still isn't getting it. "Miles, listen to me. I have feelings for someone and I'd like your blessing."

Miles stood up and pushed in his chair. "I see." The pain in his face was breaking her heart. This was the moment she'd been avoiding. "Well, I need to get back to work."

Cammie stood up and started to hug him, but stopped herself. "I'm sorry. I hope you can forgive me."

"I have to go." He turned and walked away from her, leaving her speechless.

*****

Excited to see her friend, Cammie pulled up to Dinah's two-story house, located in a cookie-cutter neighborhood called Wine Grove. There were a couple of Nerf footballs in the yard. She rang the doorbell and Dinah answered with Joey underfoot.

"Hi little guy," Cammie said to him as he ran out of the

room screaming.

Dinah rolled her eyes. "He is going through a phase. Come in."

There were toys spread out over most of the family room. Joey ran back into the room and took off his shirt and threw it at his mom.

"Joey, we wear our clothes if we are not in the bathtub. Put your shirt back on or I'm going to start counting."

The little dark-haired boy went up to his mom and took his shirt back. "Swary Mommy." He pulled on the shirt and sat down to play with one of the many toy trucks on the floor.

Dinah laughed. "Sorry about that. He's getting better. We have started doing time-outs when he misbehaves."

Cammie watched him make sound effects as he pushed his trucks in a row. She smiled. "He's cute, a handful, but cute."

Dinah nodded. "Yeah, can you believe I'm trying to have another one?"

She couldn't, but didn't say so.

Cammie looked at Dinah. "Ever since I came back home, I've felt different. Do I seem different to you?"

"A little maybe, but you're still the Cammie I adore. Just because you have had a life changing experience doesn't completely take away the person you were before."

Joey put down his truck and climbed onto Dinah's lap. "Wunch Mommy. Me Hungwey."

"Okay, let's go eat." Dinah stood up.

Cammie followed them into the kitchen.

"I made the ultimate comfort food. Homemade macaroni and cheese," Dinah said, removing the bubbling pan from the oven.

"That smells wonderful," Cammie told her.

Dinah got them all some apple cider. She put some mac and cheese in a small bowl and put it in the fridge to cool for Joey, then she dished some out in bowls for Cammie and herself.

Cammie watched her friend multi-task in awe.

Dinah put Joey in his booster seat with one hand and with the other she opened the fridge.

"You're a really good mother," Cammie told her.

"Thanks." Dinah smiled.

"I can't wait for you to meet my father and aunt. I was thinking of having Christmas at my place. Would you be able to come?"

"Sure. We do our family's celebration on Christmas eve."

*****

Cammie pulled on a sweater as she looked out the window. With Christmas only two weeks away, she had to get her decorations up. She looked at the real, blue-spruce tree she'd bought with her father last night. As she opened a box of pretty glass ornaments, she thought about what her father had asked her. He wanted her to move in with him.

She liked her house, but maybe it was time for a fresh start. Eve still hadn't found an apartment so she was staying in one of his guest rooms. Living together for a short time had given them the chance to work things out. Simon was still gone. In a way she was glad, maybe the longer he was away her feelings for him would fade.

She draped the shimmering gold ribbon down the tree. The glittery gold star she placed on top completed her decorations. Her father, Aunt Eve, Nora and Dinah's family would all come over to celebrate Christmas. She still needed to finish her shopping. She had yet to get a gift for her father. They had missed too many holidays, so she wanted to get him something he would cherish. She had also invited Miles, but he still hadn't called her back. She hoped they could be friends again someday.

Nora came through the door with a bag of groceries. "Are you ready for your lesson?"

Cammie smiled at her in the worn out apron and hoped she would like her Christmas gift. "Yes, what are we making today?"

"Lasagna."

"Thanks so much for teaching me how to cook. I enjoy it."

"You're so welcome, Dear. It has been a complete joy teaching you what I know. You're like the daughter I never had."

"And you are like a mother to me. I'm really lucky to have you in my life."

Chapter Eight

Simon sat on the log inside his hut and listened to the diamond miners on the bug he had planted earlier that week. He had come to South Africa not only to steal a red diamond, but to distance himself from Max's daughter. He still couldn't believe how close he'd come to sleeping with her. If he didn't put some space between them it was only a matter of time. He picked up a granola bar and ate it in three bites. *Why is it that I'm finally going to get my red diamond, but all I can think about are Cammie's kisses?*

*****

Cammie walked into the jewelry store on a mission to find her father a Christmas gift. After much thought, she wanted to buy a watch and have it engraved.

A middle-aged man in a pinstriped suite walked over to her. "May I help you?"

"I'm looking for a watch for my father."

He took her over to where the watches were displayed. She looked at them carefully and the one that stood out to her was gold with sapphires instead of numbers.

"Can I see that one?" She pointed to the watch.

He removed it for her and placed it in her hand. "It is one of a kind."

"It's perfect. I'll take it. Can it be engraved?"

"Of course," he said, getting out a paper and pen. "What would you like it to say?"

"All my love, Cammie."

"How nice. I wish my daughter cared about me that

much. She is a rebellious teen right now." He chuckled. "Is there anything else I can show you?"

"No that's all. Thank you." She paid for the watch and he gave her a receipt.

"We will get that engraved for you Ms. Adams and you can pick it up anytime tomorrow."

"Great, thank you. Merry Christmas," she said.

"Merry Christmas."

Cammie walked toward the door and something caught her eye, a case of loose diamonds. The heat rushed to her face and she quickly walked out the door.

When she returned home, she decided to try painting again. She started feeling the creative juices flowing so she picked up her brush and went with it. Before she even realized what she was doing, she had painted Simon's face, the same face she'd been trying to forget and it took her breath away. Seeing the loose diamonds at the jewelry store must have triggered it.

*****

Cammie took cookies out of the oven and placed them on the cooling rack. She was getting ready for her Christmas party tomorrow. As she turned off the oven, she heard the doorbell ring. She opened her door to find a shiny, green package with a big red bow. She took the package inside. The size, shape and weight felt like a canvas, which caused her heart to flip. Excited, she sat down on the sofa and carefully tore off the wrapping.

My mother's painting! She looked it over, not a scratch. She closed her eyes and smiled. *Thank you, Simon*. He hadn't forgotten. She took the painting up to her room and hung it back over her bed where it belonged. All the feelings she had been trying to ignore, flooded through her. Not caring any longer if she was broken or not, she had to see Simon somehow. Sooner the better. For the first time in her life she thought she could handle falling in love and letting someone else love her back, without fear.

*****

Christmas music played softly in the background as Cammie opened the door to the first of her guests.

Dinah came inside with Joey perched on her hip. Her husband Keith carried a bottle of wine and a stack of presents. "Merry Christmas!"

Cammie smiled warmly. "Merry Christmas."

Her father and aunt walked in right behind them. She hugged them as Nora came out of the kitchen with a tray of appetizers. She started to make introductions when the doorbell rang again. When Cammie opened the door, Miles stood there with a bag.

"Am I still welcome?" He held up the bag like it was a ticket to get inside.

She opened the door wider and smiled, happy to see her friend come around. "Always. Come in."

Cammie poured some wine and passed out glasses. The only person who could have made the evening perfect was nowhere to be found. *What would it be like to have Simon here to celebrate Christmas with?*

After the gifts were passed out, Dinah pulled Cammie aside. "Are you okay?"

"Yeah. Thanks so much for spending Christmas with my family."

"You're welcome. Thanks for having us. Though we'd

better get going, Joey needs a nap."

"Thanks for coming." She hugged her friends goodbye.

Miles took Dinah's departure as his cue to leave as well, then shortly after Eve left.

Cammie's father smiled. "Great Christmas party."

"Thanks, I'll make us some tea."

Moments later, they sat on her sofa in front of the Christmas tree's sparkling lights, sipping the hot liquid.

She tried to find the right words before speaking to her father. "I need to see Simon. I have feelings for him that are only getting stronger."

"Darling, Simon's a ladies man. He has been loyal to me, but I don't know if he has ever been loyal to a woman."

Cammie shook her head. "It doesn't matter. I have to see for myself." She paused to take another sip of her tea. "Is he coming back?"

"Eventually, he could be gone for a week or months, but I'm sure he'll come back. When he left, he said he needed a distraction. I didn't really understand what he meant at the time, but now I see."

She frowned. "Do you know where he went?"

"I have an idea. I think he may have gone to South Africa. He has a place there he likes to visit."

"I need to see him. There are some things that were not resolved when I left."

Her father sighed. "Simon's kind of unpredictable when I don't have him on my payroll."

*****

Cammie went to her father's house for breakfast. He agreed to let her take the jet to try and find Simon. As they were sitting at the kitchen island discussing the trip she was about to take, she could see Aunt Eve was not comfortable with her decision.

"Sweetie, you've been through a lot. Is it really a good idea to get involved with a guy like Simon Fisher?"

Strange to have someone tell me what to do after I practically raised myself. "I'm old enough to make my own decisions. I know what's good for me. Simon made me feel alive. I owe it to myself to see if there could be anything between us."

Eve got a stern look on her face, the way her mother used to when she misbehaved. "He's dangerous. He carries guns and likes it. I don't want to see you making the same mistakes as your mother."

Her father jumped in to save her, "In Simon's defense, he has been a dear and loyal friend to me for many years. My daughter must follow her heart."

Cammie smiled. "Aunt Eve, I'll be fine. I promise."

Eve looked over at Max and changed the subject, "I think I found an apartment. I'm going to go look at it today."

"That's wonderful," her father replied.

They finished eating in awkward silence.

Eve stood up and hugged her. "Just be careful, sweetie. I'm going to stay out of this, because I know I can't change your mind. You have your mother's strong will."

Her father stood up from the table. "You have my blessing no matter what you decide to do. You know I'm always behind you."

Cammie could understand why her aunt was worried, but she would be careful. *Who knows if I can even find Simon? He could be anywhere.*

She excused herself to go to the bathroom. On the way,

she had a sudden urge to go check out Simon's room. She stood in front of his door and turned the handle. It was unlocked, so she pushed the door open, went inside and looked around.

The bed was made, the clothes hung neatly in his closet. The lion sat majestically in front of the fireplace as if he lured her here. She touched the cool marble of his turquoise head. Something inside her took over as she pressed down to reveal Simon's collection.

She walked inside the secret room, knowing she was intruding, knowing she shouldn't be in here. She went up to the case that held all the sparkling diamonds he had once put in her hands. *So beautiful.* One or two would be pretty sure, but a couple dozen displayed together were much more compelling. She was starting to understand Simon and her parents' choice of occupation. *If it is this thrilling, just to look at them, how exciting would it be to steal them?*

Suddenly everything became crystal-clear. She had to see if being a jewel thief was something in her blood or something that she could resist and move on. She would go look for Simon and when she found him, they would complete his collection together. One of two things would happen, she would help him steal his last jewel and she would get this growing desire out of her system, or she would give into the life that she was born into. *Either way I have to know.*

*****

Cammie's father stood beside her. "Are you sure you want to do this?"

Determined, Cammie looked at her father's jet in front

of them and held on tight to her small suitcase. "I have to. I may not even find him, but I have to try." She had told him she had to figure things out, but left out the second part of her plan to help him steal a red diamond. She didn't think her father would let her go if she told him the whole truth. Since he only thought she was looking for love he more willingly told her where she might find Simon and let her use his jet to get there.

"Be safe, Darling. Call me if you run into any trouble."

Cammie hugged him goodbye. She shouldn't be afraid anymore, after all, her parents didn't die in a plane crash. Still, her heart beat wildly as she climbed the steps to the jet.

She felt less brave than she had with Aunt Eve and Simon by her side. Now she was all alone. She had no choice, if Simon really was where her father thought, in a remote area in South Africa, then she would have to fly to get there. She shut her eyes as the jet took off. She felt dizzy as she looked out the window at the horizon tilting with the trees getting smaller and smaller. She opened her eyes and took a deep breath. *Remember the reason you are doing this*.

To distract herself, she took out the art magazines that she had packed. The jet bounced up and down in some air pockets. After a few hours, she was used to the movement and relaxed a little. She let herself fall asleep.

The sound of the pilot's voice announcing they were about to land woke her up. She looked out the window and couldn't believe her eyes. No one had ever told her how beautiful and lush South Africa was. A pale-teal colored waterfall flowed over deep-dark green vegetation. *Absolute paradise.* She still couldn't believe Simon had been here before and even stayed inside an authentic African hut. Nate, her father's pilot, announced they were landing. As the jet lowered, she saw a wild elephant. It was so amazing, her mouth fell open.

Cammie stepped out of the jet into the wild terrain and was glad she bought some good boots for this trip. This was unlike any place she had ever been or dreamed of. She clung to the map her father had given her, thankful she didn't have far to go from where the jet was able to land. She just needed to walk north and she would run right into where Simon could possibly be. The thought excited her.

At least it was morning and the sun was shining. It may scary out here in darkness. It was so quiet, yet so full of sounds she had never heard. She walked bravely through the African Jungle alone. Her heart raced in anticipation of finding Simon.

A half-hour later, Cammie came upon some huts that appeared to be made of clay, logs, and straw. Like giant mushrooms. The three of them were positioned in a semi-circle with a large fire pit in the middle. Her heart skipped a beat when she saw that it had been used recently. She carefully walked up to the first of the huts and peered inside. *Empty.* She went into the next hut and found it to be empty as well. Turning to look into the last hut, she ran smack into Simon.

"Cammie! What the hell –"

She steadied herself and smiled. "Hi Simon. Fancy meeting you here."

He looked at her like he had to be hallucinating. "What are you doing here? Is everything okay? Did something happen to Max?"

She laughed at his absolute confusion. "My father is

fine. I'm here to see you."

"In that case, here I am." He put his arms around her and pulled her close.

He felt amazing. She did the right thing coming to find him. A smile plastered across her face, she wrapped her arms around him and ran her fingers through his hair. "I'm glad you didn't forget about me."

Simon kissed her hungrily and then pulled her back to look at her with serious hazel eyes. "You can't possibly be here. For sure, you can't be here kissing me."

She kissed him again, then looked into his eyes. "Everything has changed. I tried, but I couldn't get you out of my head."

"That makes two of us." Their eyes locked and he laughed. "What are you wearing?" he asked her looking at her over-the-top safari outfit, which consisted of camouflaged pants, huge boots and a straw hat.

She blushed and shrugged.

He motioned her inside the hut. "Come, welcome to my humble abode."

The inside of the hut sported a dirt floor and smelled musty. There was a big log she guessed was someplace to sit. Supplies were on a rustic table. Her eyes went to the one sleeping bag on the floor.

"You actually sleep in here?" she asked.

"Sure, I guess you could say it's like camping. I love it here. I found these huts about five years ago. They were abandoned so I claimed them as my own."

I can see why you love the land. But what about a hotel? At least for sleeping? Showering? Eating?"

"Sweetheart, this is becoming one with nature. Plus, it is very close to a diamond mine." He winked.

Now she understood. He was here for the diamonds.

Little did he know that was partly why she was here.

She bit her lip at the sound of wild animals in the distance. "It looks beautiful during the day, but at night isn't this place crawling with wildlife?"

"Don't worry. I know how to keep us safe. We'll have a fire going and remember I have guns." He smiled. "Seriously though, not that I'm not happy to see you, but why are you here? Didn't Max tell you that I'd be back?"

She smiled. *This is going to be fun.* "Well, I kind of have something that I need to get out of my system. It seems I have this brilliant idea that I want to help you acquire the red diamond for your collection."

Simon looked at her in absolute shock. "What? You're going to have to repeat that for me."

So fun. "I said I'm here to help you steal a diamond."

"What happened to, 'you're all criminals? I like safe and legal'?"

She walked around the tiny hut. "I thought about it and you said you only steal from undeserving bad people, right?"

"Yeah." He scratched his head. "I just want to finish what I started so long ago. I want that red diamond and then I'm out, for good. Are you sure, you want to do this? I can take you to a hotel to wait until I'm finished."

She looked into his eyes. "It's something I need to do. I'm scared out of my mind, but I feel I have no choice."

Simon walked over to the table. He pointed out the gear: a pair of night vision goggles, a map, a compass, flashlights, guns, a canteen, a box of canned foods and various bags of snacks. "Since I didn't know I would have company, I only packed for one. I was going to hit the diamond mine at night, when the men are asleep."

This was all starting to become very real. *Am I really*

about to do this? For real? "So what's the plan? Do you know where a red diamond is?"

"Yeah, when I first got here, I bugged one of the tents outside of the mine, at the camp where the miners stay. I have been listening to see when they had a red diamond worth stealing in their possession. This morning they finally found what I've been waiting for."

"How many guys are there? Are they dangerous?"

"There are five of them. They are armed, but more for the wildlife than anything else. Look around, we are out in the middle of nowhere. They don't suspect anyone being out here. It has been all too easy keeping tabs on them."

This was getting scary. She needed a change of subject before she lost her nerve. "Thank you for my Christmas present. It was a nice surprise."

"I got it before I came to Africa. I made sure it would be delivered on Christmas Eve."

"Thank you. I thought you'd forgotten about it. Was it difficult to find?"

"No. When you showed me the olive leaf, I knew. There's this guy named Demetrios, he lives in the states and has Greek connections. He's a thief for hire with tons of olive trees on his property. He must have been hired by the man looking for the ruby. The painting was inside his basement along with hundreds of other stolen items."

"Will he know you took it?"

He shook his head. "After I broke in and found your mother's painting, I made an anonymous call to the police. His home was raided. He was hauled away along with his truck load of stolen goods." Simon smirked.

Cammie smiled. "It means so much that you got the

painting back for me." She hugged him again. "So you've been in the jungle all this time?"

"Not exactly, I've gone to town once for food and supplies."

She nodded. "How close is the nearest town?"

"A couple of hours."

"How do you get there?"

"Follow me." He took her to the back of the biggest hut where a medium-sized safari jeep was parked.

"Is the diamond you are going to steal from someone bad?"

"Yep, it would end up in the hands of a drug lord. I'm going to make sure that doesn't happen."

"How can I help?" she asked.

"The best thing for you to do is to stay here. I don't have enough gear for both of us."

"Can we get more gear? I really want to help. I think if I can just get this out of my system I can move on. I don't always want to wonder what I am capable of, I want to know."

Simon thought for a minute. "Okay we'll go get your gear today and go over the plan. Tomorrow night we go get that diamond."

"Good, that'll give me some time to see Africa. I have never been here and it's beautiful."

"It's beautiful *and* dangerous."

She set down her suitcase and Simon looked at it. "Did you bring anything else to wear? We want to blend in and how you're dressed screams American tourist."

Cammie opened her suitcase. "I have these." She pulled out a pair of jeans and a pale yellow T-shirt. "And these." She took out a pair of tennis shoes.

"Better. You can wear your safari outfit tomorrow

night." He laughed. "We better get going so we can get back before dusk."

She changed her clothes while Simon radioed the pilot to let him know she was staying and they would be flying home late tomorrow night.

Simon helped her up into the jeep. "You're going to love this. I know where some white lions rest during the day."

She looked around trying to take everything in. It was like another world. She had to hold on not to bounce around so much. Simon drove very fast and she could tell he knew where he was going. Her hair blew all around her face. She looked over at him wearing jeans and a dark green T-shirt. His five 'o clock shadow had been replaced with dark hair which made him look rugged enough to fit in the jungle.

"Look over to the east, up under those trees." He slowed down and pointed.

About fifteen yards away she saw four white lions lounging in the sun. "They're gorgeous!"

"Yeah, they're one of my favorite things about coming here." After a few minutes, he sped the jeep up again.

She was speechless the rest of the way to town. The tall grass gracefully swayed in the wind. Every so often, she could see little creatures curiously poking their heads out of the grass to watch them. The closer they got to town, the less lush the landscape.

Chapter Nine

Cammie was impressed how well Simon knew his way around and where to get the things she would need. The town was hectic, nothing like where they were just two hours ago. Most of the people Simon dealt with spoke English, but had such a strong accent she had trouble keeping up. They got what they needed and didn't linger.

Simon helped her back into the jeep. "I still can't believe you're here."

She smiled. "Neither can I."

"Is Max going to kill me when I get back?"

She laughed. "No. He's skeptical, but okay with it." It would be dark soon and the bugs were already starting to bite. Feeling a sting, she slapped her arm. "I hate bugs, but they seem to *love* me."

Simon laughed. "Because you taste delicious."

She shook her head and smiled. Straight ahead, she saw another elephant meandering. The only elephants and lions she had ever seen were at the zoo.

She let out a sigh of relief when they got back to the huts before dark. Simon took everything they had gotten inside, then started a fire.

"Are you hungry?" he asked.

"Yeah. What do we have to eat?"

He looked inside the box, which held the remainder of his food supply. "Your choices are beans or soup."

Cammie scrunched her nose. "Men and beans don't mix. I'll go with soup."

Simon laughed. "Chicken noodle or vegetable beef."

"Either is fine."

"Okay, we'll have vegetable beef."

She took the cans from him. "Let me."

"Really? Are you sure? There's not a microwave out here."

"Ha ha. I'll have you know, Nora has given me cooking lessons. I have the basics down at least."

"A sexy cook, how lucky am I?" He smiled.

"Pretty, damn lucky." She took the can opener, twisted open two cans of soup and poured them in a pan.

Simon moved her hair to the side and kissed the back of her neck. "I agree."

She smiled and looked through the other food. *He packed marshmallows?* She had to hold in a giggle. *Tough jungle man eats marshmallows.*

She held out the bag. "We have to roast these for dessert."

"Sounds good to me."

She waited for the fire to die down, then put the soup on. After dinner, Simon found a couple sticks for the marshmallows. He roasted one for her. She slipped the hot, gooey mess off the stick and burned her finger in the process.

"Ouch!"

Simon sat down his stick and looked at her sticky, red finger. He put her finger in his mouth and sucked off the goo. "Better?"

"Yes," she said, breathless.

Cammie bagged up the dishes. "Where do you wash out the pan and bowls?"

"There's a waterfall not far from here. We can wash them out in the morning."

"Okay."

Simon made sure the fire was going strong again. When it got dark, Cammie looked out at the sky. She had never seen so many stars so bright. It felt like if she reached far enough she just might be able to touch one.

"Amazing, isn't it?" Simon asked.

"Yeah, it is."

"We better go inside and get some sleep. We have a lot to go over in the morning.

She quickly made a wish on the brightest star that tomorrow would go smoothly. "Okay."

They took everything inside the hut and Simon closed the door. He lit a lantern. Cammie packed light, so she just slipped off her jeans and stayed in her T-shirt. He walked over to the sleeping bag and unzipped it.

"Sorry we don't have a bed." He patted the sleeping bag. She walked over and climbed in beside him. *How am I going to get any sleep sharing a sleeping bag with Simon?*

He put his arms around her and pulled her close. "You have no idea how bad I have wanted to do this." His tongue parted her lips.

"I think I have a pretty good idea." She kissed him slow and deep, until the sleeping bag got steamy hot. They pulled off their clothes and tossed them out of the bag. He kissed her neck and then moved down to her chest. She grabbed a hold of his hair and moaned. Closing his eyes, he rolled her on top of him and his cocky smiled changed into a smile she had never seen before, one of complete satisfaction.

*****

Simon glanced over at Cammie and smiled. Not only was she here in Africa, with him, she wanted to help him steal the red diamond. What he'd done to deserve such luck he had no idea, but for the first time in a long time he was happy. He just hoped he could live up to who she thought him to be.

*****

The bright African sun had them both awake at the crack of dawn. "You want to go for a run down to the waterfall?" Simon asked.

"Are you kidding? Yes! Let's go."

They got dressed and grabbed the dishes.

"It's not too far, maybe twenty minutes." Simon unloaded his gun and put the bullets inside his pocket. He tucked his gun in the back of his pants. "Don't run with a loaded gun." He winked.

Cammie smiled and nodded. A thought occurred to her. "Simon, have you ever killed anyone?" She held her breath waiting for his response.

"Wounded yes, killed no."

She exhaled relieved.

"Follow me and try to keep up," he joked.

Cammie was so excited to be running, especially with Simon. The waterfall was not far, just as he'd promised. It must have been at least fifty feet high. The water was such a beautiful color, crystal-clear with a teal tint as the sun danced across it.

"I just run the dishes under the waterfall. It does a decent job."

After they got the dishes clean, she bagged them back up.

Cammie stuck her foot in the water. "Do you want to go in?"

"Well, it is probably the only shower we're going to get."

They took off their clothes and swam over to the

middle of the fall. The refreshing water poured over their naked bodies. They made love for a second time in the jungle.

As they were swimming back to get dressed, a large, colorful bird swooped down and chirped at them, making them both laugh. Cammie's hair hung in long waves dripping wet. She tried to wring her hair out the best she could. Simon just shook his head like a dog and it fell perfectly back into place.

The African heat had dried them by the time they reached the hut. Cammie dug through her suitcase and found her brush and lip-gloss.

Her stomach growled. "What do we have for breakfast?"

"I think there are some granola and breakfast bars in there."

She got two breakfast bars out of the box and handed one to Simon.

"So are you really ready for tonight? Any second thoughts?" he asked.

"No second thoughts, I'm ready," she said, sure of her decision.

Simon went over all the gear. He showed her how to hold a gun again and how to use the night goggles.

"Just stay close to me and do exactly as I tell you. I don't foresee any problems. This should be one of my easier jobs now that they have the diamond. The hardest part has been the waiting."

Cammie nodded. She tried to remember everything he told her. She wanted to get that diamond so they could both get stealing jewels out of their systems. Ironically, she wasn't even afraid. *Maybe that will change tonight.*

"So you want to go on safari?" he asked.

"Sounds like fun."

They got into the jeep and Simon pointed out animals as they drove by.

Cammie wished she would have brought a camera. The sky went on forever out here. The sun looked so much bigger and lower here than she had ever seen. Simon took her back to see the white lions again. She gazed at a lion licking his creamy white fur. Another one lying next to him yawned.

"They remind me of the lion statue in your room."

Simon nodded. "This is where I got him."

"Wow, it came all the way from Africa?"

"Yeah, I've had him for about five years. Lions are my favorite animal. Especially, the white ones."

"I think after seeing them, they're mine too." She smiled.

Simon turned the jeep around and headed back. He passed Cammie some water. She gave it back to him and he took a long drink.

They ate lunch and took a nap. Cammie opened her eyes and saw Simon gazing at her like she was beautiful, she liked it a lot. He kissed her nose and smiled.

"Hey, sorry I slept so long," she told him.

Nodding, he got up and stretched. "It's all the fresh air. It makes you sleepy."

She followed him and yawned. "I never would've thought I could sleep so well on the ground."

"You would be surprised what you can do. We better eat and have everything packed and ready to go. When we get the diamond, we'll come here to get the jeep. We'll take the jeep back to town where I borrowed it and call the pilot. We need to be ready to move fast. I want to be in the air by the time they wake up and realize the diamond is gone.

"Okay," she said, making more soup.

"I can't wait to get back, so you can try out your new cooking skills on me. I have been living off beans and soup for too long."

"I don't know how you did it. I'm already sick of soup. You know what sounds really good is that fast food you're so fond of."

"Mmm, I could use some grease."

Chapter Ten

Heart pounding, Cammie followed Simon through the dark jungle with a loaded gun in her hand. Amazing how good she could see with the night vision goggles on. They'd listened to the chatter on Simon's bug until the guys fell asleep. Simon knew exactly where he was going and knew where the diamond was kept. The moon and stars were the only illumination in dark jungle. Wild animals howled in the distance. *I hope they stay on their side of the jungle.*

Simon stopped and turned around. "Are you okay back there?"

"Yeah. Maybe adventure really is in my blood."

He smiled. "It's not much farther. When we get there, we're going into the tent I told you about. There will be a large wooden box. The diamonds are inside. Once I get the lock open, you take the red diamond. It will be the largest one. Take nothing else. Remember we have to get in, get what we came for and get out. If anything happens, you take that diamond and run back to the jeep, no matter what."

She took a deep breath. "Okay."

They walked about five more yards and then she saw a dying fire. Thanks to the goggles, she spied the tent that Simon had told her about. It was the closest one to the entrance of the mine. It was hard to grip the gun with her clammy hands. Five other tents circled around the fire. Simon motioned for her to follow him around the back of the tents. They arrived at the tent she was to go inside.

Simon gave her a quick peck on the lips and nodded. They went inside the tent. Simon got the box open within a few seconds. She felt like she couldn't breathe when she looked into the wooden box almost full of clear loose diamonds. Resting on top was the red diamond, by far the largest diamond inside the box.

Adrenaline took over. She picked up the gem and put it into her pocket, careful not to drop the gun. It was surprisingly easy to take something that wasn't hers. As Simon locked the box back, they heard one of the men get up. Simon grabbed her and they went behind the tent. They squatted down low and peeked around. One of the men had gotten up to pee. They held their breath in the dark, waiting. Cammie was sure the beat of her heart was loud enough for the guy to hear.

When the guy went back inside his tent, she took a step to follow Simon and accidentally stepped on a large twig. The loud crack sounded through the silent, night air. She froze. They heard someone coming out of their tent. Simon grabbed her hand and pulled her into the mine shaft to hide. The mine was damp with an earthy smell. Tracks with rickety old carts lined the middle of the tunnel. On the opposite side of them were dirt-covered shovels, buckets and round shifters. *Damn! We would be on our way back to the huts right now, if I hadn't stepped on that stupid twig.*

They pressed their bodies flat to the rock wall as they listened. When the voices got closer, Simon took her hand and pulled her farther into the mine. Her feet sunk down into the deep mud. She felt gritty gravel at the bottom of the sludge. *Thank goodness, we're equipped with boots and night vision goggles.* They went a little deeper into the mine.

Simon stopped to listen. Men's voices carried through the tunnel. "Shit. I think we're going to have to find another way out. We don't have much time to get out of here. If they check the box and see the red diamond is missing, they will search the area. We need them to think one of their own stole the diamond."

Cammie wanted to cry. *Why did I even come? Now we're both in danger.* She pressed her lips together to hold in the emotion that threatened to escape.

Simon put his hands on her shoulders. "We're going to find a way out, okay? I need you to trust me." She swallowed and nodded. Afraid for both their lives, she followed him with her feet growing heavy from the wet mud that now clung to her boots and pants. The air was thick the farther they got, making it difficult to breathe.

"Look." Simon pointed to a round opening in the ground to the right of them. It must have been ten feet wide and twenty feet deep. The bottom of the pit looked like gravel. He took out a small flashlight and shined it down into the hole. She looked down at what she had thought was gravel. Among the little rocks was what looked like dirty chunks of ice.

"Diamonds." Various shapes and sizes mixed in with worthless rocks. He shut the flashlight off and they continued through.

Cammie stepped on something crunchy. She looked down and screamed. Simon put his hand over her mouth. He looked down to see what caused her alarm.

"Is that human?" she asked, looking down at half a rib cage.

He hugged her tight. "I think so. Come on, I'm getting you out of here." There was a small path to their left. Simon stopped. "I feel air. This way." The opening was so narrow they had to turn sideways to get through.

About ten minutes later, they were out of the mine

somewhere in the jungle. Cammie inhaled a big gulp of the fresh air and Simon took off his backpack. She watched him dig through the supplies with his light.

"Here it is." He held up a compass. "Do you need a drink?" He handed her the canteen.

"Yeah, but I think I need something stronger than water right now." She took a drink anyway and handed it back to him.

"We're okay. We need to head east. We should only be about an hour out of our way."

Cammie nodded and tried to be brave even though she felt sweaty, dirty and sick of being brave. Her pants were damp and her night vision goggles were heavy. The bugs in the jungle were having a feast on her skin. Somehow, she never pictured this part of stealing a diamond. The wild noises of the inhabitants echoed around them. She didn't want to shoot an animal, but she would if they decided she looked tasty.

They moved swiftly through the darkness toward the huts. By the time they got back, she was out of breath. She jumped in the jeep, relieved.

Simon gave her a quick kiss. "You were amazing. Now let's get out of here."

She gripped the jeep handle as they sped through the darkness.

"That was close."

Close is an understatement. "Yeah, you think they know the diamond is missing, yet?"

"Hard to say. You did it. How do you feel?"

She shook her head. "I feel crazy. I feel a rush like I have never felt before."

"Your first heist. It's your diamond," Simon told her.

"No, it's yours, for your collection," she said.

"How about a compromise. We share it."
Cammie smiled. "Sharing's good."

*****

Inside the jet, Cammie could see how dirty they had gotten. *A hot shower would feel great right now.* She would have to settle for wiping off the best she could with a bottle of water and napkins. Once they were in the air, Simon asked her to take the diamond out. She took it out of her pocket and gasped at the huge red rock.

"It's stunning," Simon said, as she handed it to him. He examined it and whistled. "Well done, my little jewel thief."

Cammie laughed, uneasy. "I couldn't have done it without you."

Simon handed the diamond back to her. "You hold onto it."

She put it back into her pocket. The diamond was gorgeous, but when she pulled it out of her pocket, she'd had a flashback of the ruby.

"I feel sick now," she told him.

He held her hand. "That's normal. It'll be okay."

She bit her lip and looked out the window. "Are you sure they won't come looking for us?"

"There is no possible way they can. They have no idea what just hit them. Most likely, they'll blame one of their own, thinking they took it while the others slept. That's why we only took the one diamond."

She felt a little better. "Um, maybe we shouldn't tell my father about this."

"Are you kidding? He may want to kill me, but you

shouldn't keep secrets from him. That is the one thing you were most angry with him for."

He's right. "That was a one time thing for me."

Simon looked at her. "Are you sure?"

She didn't hesitate. "Positive. I think I just wanted to see what it was like. I wanted to see how my mother felt, just once."

"I'm done too. I had a good run. Now, I am ready to quit. This time wasn't as thrilling for me. For the first time ever, I had something to lose and I didn't like that feeling."

Her heart melted and she took his hand. "Aww...thanks, Simon."

He squeezed her fingers. "No, Sweetheart, thank you."

*****

After landing, Simon got a rental car. "Now let's go get some real food."

Her stomach growled. "Sounds good."

He pulled over to the first burger joint they came across and ordered cheeseburgers, fries, and large chocolate shakes. Fast food never tasted so good.

When they arrived back at her father's estate, Cammie was relieved that he wasn't home. She looked for Eve, but she wasn't there either. She followed Simon to his room and handed him the red diamond. He placed the diamond in the glass case with all the others.

"It's complete. Finally, after ten years." Simon rubbed his thumb against her cheek. "Thanks for helping me."

"You're welcome." The diamonds didn't seem as irresistible as they did before. Their pull on her was gone. The only thing she could not resist in this room was Simon Fisher. They walked out of the room and Simon closed the faux door.

Simon took her hand and led her to the shower. The water turned black from the mud that washed off them. Cammie massaged the conditioner into her hair. After her hair was rinsed, Simon turned her around and lifted her to him. She wrapped her legs around him as he pressed her to the wall. Their bodies moved together rhythmically in the cascade of water. She hung on to him and cried out in pleasure. Smiling, he carefully put her back down. They got out and dried off, still feeling euphoric.

She dried her hair. "It feels so good to have my hair clean."

"And it smells good," Simon said.

She laughed. "You smell pretty good yourself." His rugged jungle smell was replaced by his spicy-cinnamon-citrus cologne she found irresistible.

"I don't have any clean clothes here."

"You can put something of mine on and make a run for it before anyone gets home."

She frowned. "You trying to get rid of me already?"

He pulled her to him. "Does this feel like I want to get rid of you?"

She shook her head and smiled. "My father asked me to move in. What would you think about that?"

He tilted her chin up, so her eyes met his eyes. "I think I would like that. Let's go get your stuff so you can stay here *tonight*."

"Right now?"

He smirked. "I'm ready. Are you?"

Cammie swallowed hard. *Am I?* "I'd have my own room of course."

"And I'd be right down the hall if you wanted to sleep over." He winked and slapped her butt. She got dressed in a pair of Simon's sweat pants and a T-shirt.

They got into her Lexus and she drove to her house. She would have to put her house up for sale.

Simon followed her into the house. "Nice place."

"Yeah, it's not as extravagant as my father's, but it's nice." She took out some bags and filled them up with clothes and personal items. "This is enough for tonight. Tomorrow I'll call a moving company."

*****

Now he'd done it. He'd have to find a way to tell Max. Simon hoped his friend would give them his blessing. He would not cause trouble between Cammie and her father. The bad thing was he didn't want to think about her not being in his life. He knew she was dangerous from the minute he'd looked into those big, blue eyes. *She may still be the death of me.*

*****

They had gotten home late last night. Her father didn't even know they were there. Cammie peeked out Simon's door to see if she could hear anyone in the house. She wrapped the towel tightly around her and ran down the hall to her new room. She found a red shirt-dress and slipped it on. She fixed her hair and put on some makeup. Simon had seen her at her worst for a couple of days. She wanted to look her best for him now.

They'd been through so much together. She had a hard time remembering life without him. She felt like she was floating, maybe she was starting to fall in love. Maybe it was time to tell him she was a PI, well sort of. She'd never really started her business.

She found Simon downstairs in the living room, clean-shaven, on the sofa dressed in a white button down shirt and dark jeans. He whistled at her when she walked into the room. Heat rose to her cheeks. *How does he still have that effect on me?*

Cammie grinned. "You're not so bad yourself."

"It feels good to be back. This sofa feels unbelievably soft."

"Well, you did sleep on the ground for over week," she reminded him.

"So how are we going to break the news to your father?"

"Which news? That we're together or that I had my first heist?" She giggled.

"Maybe you better start with the diamond." He winked.

"My father adores you, Simon. I'm sure you have nothing to worry about."

"Yeah, he adores me as a friend, not so sure he'll like the fact that I'm sleeping with his daughter."

As if right on cue, Max and Eve walked in. "Darling, you're back! And I see you brought Simon back with you."

"Glad you're home safe," Eve told her.

"Thanks. It's good to be back."

"Hey, you'll never believe –"

Cammie gave Simon a warning look. She didn't want her aunt to find out what she'd done. "That I'm not afraid of flying anymore!"

"That's great. How was Africa?" her father asked.

"Wonderful. It's such a beautiful place. Simon took me

on safari and you wouldn't believe how close we got to a few white lions."

"That's fantastic." He nodded at Simon, "Thank you for taking care of my daughter once again."

"Happy to." Simon turned and winked at Cammie.

She looked at her father. "I've given it a lot of thought and I've decided I will move in. You did go through all the trouble of making a beautiful room for me."

He smiled and hugged her. "Welcome home, Darling!"

"Speaking of moving, I've been looking for an apartment without any luck," Eve said.

Cammie thought for a minute. "Why don't you live at The Kipton?"

"Would that be too strange?" Eve asked.

Cammie shook her head. "Not at all, it is a beautiful place to live and much better than any apartment."

Eve nodded. "Okay."

Simon pulled Max aside while Cammie talked to her aunt. She watched them shake hands from across the room. "I'll call Miles for you. I know you'll be welcome there."

"Okay, I just can't bring myself to live alone after everything that happened."

She could see being abducted was much harder on her aunt than it had been on her. After all, she had Simon to help her through it.

Max and Eve went upstairs.

"What were you and my father talking about over here?" she asked Simon.

"I asked him permission to date you."

Cammie laughed. "Oh yeah, and what did he say?"

"He said he was done trying to protect you and gave me his blessing...with a warning attached."

"I'm glad he realizes that I can take care of myself."

"As much as I want to, I don't think we should sleep in the same bed under your father's roof. I don't want to disrespect him."

"Nor do I. I'm fine with sleeping in my own room, for now." She smiled.

"Agreed."

She took his hands. "This is a little bizarre us dating and living together in my father's house."

"It is, but we can take things slow."

"Perfect. My life has been on fast forward ever since we met. Now I would just like to pause for while and enjoy having everyone back in my life safe. I need to call Miles for Eve. She may move into The Kipton."

Simon kissed her lips. "Go call Miles. I'll be in my room."

Cammie went into her room and picked up the phone. "Hi, it's Cammie."

"Hi, how are you?" Miles asked.

"I'm fine. Hey, my Aunt Eve has been looking for someplace to live without any luck. Do you have any resident suites available?"

"Yes, I'll take care of her. Send her in any time."

"Wonderful, thank you. Take care." Cammie hung up the phone.

She went down the hall to Simon's room and knocked on the door.

"Come in." He was watching TV, which he turned off as she entered. She sat down on the loveseat beside him and he put his arm around her. "What did he say?"

"He said she could move in. Eve will love it there. It's beautiful and safe. The only reason I didn't like living at The Kipton was that it reminded me of my parents' deaths."

"I am glad I met you." He kissed her.

"Me too." She let go of him and stood up. "I need to call a moving company and a realtor."

"Is there anything you want to go get now?"

This is really happening. "Maybe some of my artwork."

Simon stood up. "Let's go."

Chapter Eleven

Cammie pulled her Lexus into her driveway behind Nora's car. It was bizarre how her father's estate already felt like home. This house was just a house now.

Nora opened the door. "I was just leaving, Dear."

She went inside. "Can you stay for a few minutes? There's something I need to talk to you about."

"Of course." She smiled. They all went into the living room and sat down on the sofa.

Cammie put her hand on Simon's shoulder. "This is Simon, the man who rescued me."

Simon nodded and smiled. "I've heard wonderful things about you."

Nora smiled. "And I you."

"I've decided to move in with my father. He has an enormous house. It kind of looks like a castle."

Nora nodded. "How lovely that you can be close to him."

"I would like for you to come work for me at my father's estate. Since it is a considerable drive, you can move in if you like. You would have your own room. It wouldn't be quite as big as your place at The Kipton, but almost. You would have to share the kitchen, but you would have enough room for a sofa and TV in your room. I don't want you to feel like you have to by any means, but the offer is there if you are interested."

"I do not even have to think about it, Dear. I would love to."

"Wonderful! When I have the movers come to get the rest of my things, I'll have them send someone for yours, also. How soon would you like to come?"

"Anytime is fine with me."

"Okay by the end of the week then? You don't have to pack anything. The movers will do that for you."

"Well, okay," Nora said.

"Don't worry about cleaning this house anymore." She took out a notepad and pen. "Here are the directions to our new place." She handed her the paper.

"I'll see you next week." Nora hugged her and left.

Simon followed Cammie through the house to the back door and they went out to her studio.

He looked around. "Wow, you painted all these?"

"Yes. This one has become my favorite." She walked over and picked up the painting of Simon's face.

"I'm flattered. When did you do this?"

"Right before Christmas. I tried really hard to forget about you. One day when I starting painting, my subconscious must have taken over, because this is what I ended up painting." She paused to look into his eyes. "You are the first *person* I had ever painted."

"You're really talented. I'm glad you couldn't completely forget about me anymore than I could forget about you."

"Me too. I feel like my life has just started. I was in such a bad place when I met Miles. He gave me comfort. When I met you, you woke me up. I felt alive for the first time since my parents' deaths. I think that when their plane crashed a big part of me died with it. Now I not only have my father back, I have a part of myself I did not even realize was there."

Simon hugged her and kissed her head.

"I want to get my mother's painting. It's in my bedroom."

He carried the painting and followed her inside. She

carefully took the painting down that was hung over her bed.

"I'm going to grab some more clothes and I'll be ready."

He nodded. "I'll take these to the car."

She grabbed her suitcase and filled it with as many clothes as she could.

*****

Cammie opened the door for Simon so he could carry her paintings upstairs. Her father was in the living room reading. She sat down next to him as Simon came back downstairs.

"There's something I wanted to tell you. I just saw Nora. You remember her from Christmas?"

Her father looked up. "Yes, remarkable woman."

"Well, I talked her into coming to live here to be our housekeeper. I thought she could have the largest guest room by the library."

A slight smile formed on her father's lips. "Wonderful, I would love to have Nora here."

Cammie's eyebrows rose. "You would?"

"Yes, we had a nice conversation at Christmas," he said.

Simon chuckled quietly.

"She must have been quite the conversationalist," Cammie told him.

Her father smiled. "Please tell her to make herself at home." He walked away.

Cammie's eyes followed her father and then turned to Simon. "Did you see that?"

"Yeah, that's the first time I have ever seen Max smile about any woman, unless he was talking about your mother."

"Well, it has been seven years. I think he's grieved enough."

"This should be interesting." Simon smirked.

"You know, I thought that Nora was so quick to say yes because of me, but now I wonder if my father had a little something to do with it. I was so preoccupied at Christmas I didn't even pay attention to the two of them talking," Cammie said, shaking her head.

"They'd be cute together."

"Yeah, they would." She paused and smiled. "Wait until I tell Dinah! She's been telling Nora she should date. I need to call her. I haven't even told her I'm moving."

"Tell me more about Dinah," Simon said.

"She's great. I met her at The Kipton when I was sixteen. We have stayed friends over the years. Now she is married to a policeman, has a two year old son and is pregnant."

"I promised your father I'd help him out with something tomorrow, maybe you could go see her," Simon suggested.

"What are you helping him with?"

"Just a new hobby he's picked up."

Cammie pursed her lips. "Nothing illegal is it?"

"Nope. Something called Geocaching, a sort of hide and seek for adults."

"Okay. I'll see if she's free. If not, I can probably persuade her with food. She's always hungry now."

"Speaking of being hungry, what are we going to eat for dinner?"

"It's a surprise. Go visit with my father and I'll let you guys know when dinner is ready."

"Can't wait."

Cammie took out her cookbook she had taken from the

house, the one that Nora had bought for her. She looked over the index until she found it, then turned to the page that had the recipe for filet mignon. After the steak was baking, she decided to make potatoes as well.

Once the steaks were almost done, Eve wandered into the kitchen. "What smells so delicious?"

"I'm making dinner...Filet Mignon with mushroom gravy and baked potatoes."

"That sounds wonderful. Do you need any help?"

"Sure, you can add some peppers to the salad." Cammie washed her hands. "Guess what? Good news! I talked to Miles and he has an empty suite for you, if you want it."

"Really?" Eve smiled as she diced orange bell peppers.

"Yes. You are going to go live at the Kipton and Nora is going to come live here."

Eve laughed. "Am I getting her suite then?"

"I don't think so."

"How soon can I move?"

"Whenever you want. I'm having a mover get the rest of my things and Nora's by the end of the week."

Eve tossed the peppers into the salad. "So how are things with Simon?"

Cammie grinned. "Can't you tell?"

"I'm glad you're happy. Just be careful. He seems like a nice guy, but he still makes me nervous."

The timer for the steaks went off. Cammie put on potholders and took them out. She looked over at Eve. "You want to tell the guys dinner is ready?"

"Sure." Eve went and to get them.

"Darling, I am impressed," her father told her, sitting down at the table.

Simon cut into his steak and took a bite. "This is

amazing. It's the best filet mignon I've ever eaten."

Cammie grinned. "Thanks."

"This is delicious, great job," Eve told her.

They devoured Cammie's meal. When they were finished, Eve told her she would clean up. Simon snuck Cammie up to his room where they cuddled up on his loveseat and made out like teenagers.

"I guess I should call Dinah and go to bed."

"You, me, same place, tomorrow night?" Simon kissed her again.

"It's a date. Goodnight."

He winked. "Goodnight."

Cammie walked down the hall to her room. She picked up the phone and called her best friend. "Hey, it's Cammie."

"Hi! How are you? Anything new?" Dinah asked.

"So much. I was wondering if you could meet me at my father's tomorrow. It's my turn to make lunch."

"Um, hold on. Okay, yes I can. Keith is off work so he can take care of Joey. Can you email me the directions?"

"Yes, come around noon if you can."

"Okay, see you tomorrow."

Cammie got into bed and smiled. *I'm finally right where I belong.*

Chapter Twelve

For the second time in Simon's life, he felt cared about. The first time had been when Max took him under his wing and kept him out of trouble. Simon's own parents were the ones who first got him *into* trouble. Now, he knew Cammie cared about him. He had her figured all wrong, she wasn't spoiled. She was compassionate. Now that he'd felt what it was like to be cared about by a woman, he was terrified of ever losing that feeling. *Falling in love is an even bigger rush than stealing jewels.*

*****

When Cammie woke up, the house was quiet. Eve was touring The Kipton, Simon and her father were out. Dinah would be coming to visit at noon.

After running, Cammie tidied up her room, then took a shower. Thanks to grabbing more clothes yesterday, she had more choices. She went into the closet and picked a pair of white-denim shorts and a peacock-inspired, sleeveless shirt. After brushing her hair, she put on her taupe eye shadow and lip-gloss.

Cammie made pasta with roasted vegetables and homemade bread sticks for lunch. She was just taking the bread sticks out of the oven when Dinah arrived at the gate.

"I'm here," Dinah said, through the intercom.

Cammie opened the gate. "Okay, pull up to the garage."

Dinah pulled her minivan up and Cammie met her outside. "Wow, are you kidding me? Look at this place. It looks like a castle right out of a fairytale."

"I know. It does, doesn't it?" Cammie grinned. She led Dinah to the front door. "You look great."

Dinah patted her belly. "Thanks, I'm starting to feel big." Not only was Dinah glowing, she looked cute in her knit maternity sundress.

"Let me show you around my new home."

"I can't wait," Dinah squealed.

After she walked Dinah through the entire house, Cammie and Dinah sat at the kitchen island eating pasta and bread sticks. Cammie filled Dinah in on all that had happened since they had last spoken. She left out the part about the diamond as she had with her father and Eve. Dinah did not seem as surprised as Cammie thought she would be.

"I kind of saw this coming. The way you lit up when you talked about Simon was obvious."

Cammie nodded. "I think everything is working out."

"The baby loves your pasta," Dinah said, taking her second helping.

Cammie laughed.

"How serious is it with Simon?"

Cammie set down her glass. "We've agreed to take it slow. I feel like I'm just getting my life back. I just want to take my time and enjoy everything."

"So, you think your father likes Nora?"

"I think so. I can't wait until she moves in to see if she likes him, too. That would be nice for them. They have both been alone for so long."

"Well, I really like your... uh, castle, house, whatever."

"Thanks. You'll have to come back soon to watch a movie in the theatre."

Cammie cleared the dishes and told her friend goodbye. After Dinah left she went outside to the pond and sat down on the dock. She thought about the memories her and Simon had already created there. A few minutes later, Simon walked up behind her and sat down next to her.

"How was Geocaching?" she asked.

He shrugged. "Your father really seems to like it."

"I had a nice lunch with Dinah. She wasn't all that shocked that we're together."

"Neither am I," Simon said, taking her hand.

She smiled. "I have an idea."

Simon licked his lips. "So do I."

She laughed. "Not that. I have a proposition for you."

Simon tilted his head. "I'm listening."

"I just got my PI license before we met. And I could use a partner. It would be legal, but dangerous enough to keep you satisfied. I think we'd make a great team."

"No shit?" He paused. "You're a PI?"

She nodded. "Well, technically, I haven't had my first case."

Simon shook his head. "You amaze me and I think we would make a great team."

She smiled. "Good. I thought my father could handle the paperwork. We could each put in an equal financial share so we would all own a piece of the business."

Simon wrapped his arms around her. "One condition, I get to teach you self-defense."

"Agreed."

He whispered in her ear, "I'm going to have so much fun teaching you everything I know."

She stood up. "Later, let's go run this by my father and see if he's interested."

They went into the house to find her father in the library reading.

He put down his book.

Cammie began, “There’s something I would like to talk to you about.”

“Okay.”

“I got my PI license before I was abducted. I’ve asked Simon to be my partner and I was wondering if you wanted in as a silent partner?”

Her father had a pained look on his face. “Can’t you do something less dangerous, like paint?”

“Simon will teach me self-defense and how to be sneaky.”

Max sighed. “That, Darling, is what frightens me.”

Simon looked at Cammie. “Can I tell him about Africa?” Cammie nodded. “Cammie did something with me in Africa that was all her decision. And she handled herself perfectly...she stole a four-carat red diamond.”

Her father's face turned red as he looked at Cammie. “You did what?”

“It’s okay. Simon was there in case anything happened. I just wanted to see what it felt like. I wanted to see what drew all of you to stealing jewels. I have to say it was a rush, but it’s not something I really want to do again. At least being a PI is *legal*.”

Her father took a deep breath. “I see you have your mother’s strong will. I’m in.”

She hugged him, relieved.

“One thing, Darling. I want to take you on a short trip first.”

“Okay. When we get back, Simon can start teaching me self-defense.”

“Wonderful. Can you excuse us a moment, Darling?”

“Okay. If this is about me though, I have a right to be here,” she said.

Her father paused. "Very well, I was just going to ask Simon why he failed to mention the red diamond to me before."

"It wasn't my place to tell you. It was Cammie's."

Max sighed. "I guess I am going to have to get used to you dating my daughter."

"Let's go downstairs and open a bottle of wine to celebrate our new business," Cammie said, changing the subject.

"You two go ahead, I'm going to do some more reading. I need to finish planning our father-daughter trip."

Cammie and Simon went back downstairs to the kitchen. Simon opened a bottle of red wine and toasted to their new business and partnership.

*****

Simon pulled her closer to him in the bed. His warm, strong body made her feel protected maybe even loved, though neither of them had said the L-word, yet. Cammie wouldn't be the first to say it. She didn't want to scare Simon away. But she did love him, more than anything. She kissed his hand intertwined with hers and fell asleep with a smile on her face.

*****

Cammie finished packing, excited for her trip. She would miss Simon, but she really needed this time with her father. They had lost out on seven years of each other's lives. She lugged her bag downstairs and hugged Simon goodbye.

"Don't forget about me while I'm gone," she told him.

"Not a chance." He kissed her lips. "Have a great time with your father. I'll try to find a location for our office while you're gone."

Cammie waved and got into her father's luxury SUV. Her father backed out of the garage and out of the gate.

"I must confess something. I may have used Geocaching as an excuse to spend time with my daughter."

She smiled. "You don't have to use an excuse for us to spend time together. I'm looking forward to it."

Her father looked over at her. "I'm glad to hear that. We haven't really had a chance to catch up."

"I know. Things have been crazy."

"There are three places I want to visit with you. One place just happens to have a hidden cache so we can check that out if you want."

"Sure. What three places?"

"A surprise. Are you in a hurry to get back?"

"No, like I said, I'm happy to spend some time with you."

"How are things with Simon?"

"Great." She paused. "He hasn't told me anything about his past or how you two met."

"Give him time."

She had hoped to get the story from her father, but she didn't press.

As her father drove, Cammie started to recognize where they were. It was the area where she grew up in. As soon as she saw the art museum, she smiled. It was the place that first got her interested in painting. Her mother and father had taken her there when she was eleven. A week after she had gotten hurt on her skateboard, her parents tried to get her interested in a new hobby.

They had walked her through the museum and let her look at all the many forms of art. It was Cammie that became obsessed with the paintings. Her parents went and bought her first set of oil paints that night.

Her father parked in the parking garage.

"I haven't been here since I was fourteen."

"I remember how thrilled your mother and I were when you took an interest in painting. Art was a much safer hobby than skateboarding."

They walked into the modern building. The architecture itself was a piece of art. She loved the smell of the building, like her art classroom in grade school. There were a lot of new paintings since she'd been here. She walked slowly through, appreciating the talent that hung upon the walls.

When she came to her favorite painting, the one that first inspired her, she stopped. Her father sat down on the bench in front of the painting. He motioned for her to sit beside him. They sat and gazed at the famous work of art, which was a gorgeous man, handing a beautiful woman, a ruby necklace. The love in their eyes was so compelling you hardly noticed they were nude.

She got chills. It was as if she was seeing the painting through different eyes. "A ruby necklace, I never really saw the necklace until just now." *How did I not remember that?*

Her father nodded. "Your mother and I thought it was a sign. Out of all the art and all the paintings in this building, that was your favorite."

Cammie didn't know what to say. She gazed at the painting, speechless. She suddenly felt a presence like her mother was there with them. She could almost feel her warm arms around her. Cammie smiled, as a tear slid down her cheek.

"Thank you for bringing me here," she said, standing up. "Where to next?"

"Would you like to see the place your mother and I had our first heist?"

"I think I would." She followed him back to the SUV.

"It's a long drive. We will have to stay at a hotel tonight after we visit."

Cammie nodded. Things in her life were piecing together like a puzzle that had always had a few missing pieces. She wanted to know and understand who she was and where she came from. Finally, she would be free of the secrets that always kept her from her true self.

Her father pulled into a large parking lot. She looked up at the large fancy building. The sign read, ELEGANT GEMSTONE COMPANY. There were two small fountains on either side of the glass revolving door. As soon as she got up to the door, she could hear soft, classical music playing. They went inside the huge showroom. Cammie could see why her parents choose this place for their first heist. Diamonds, precious gemstones, and gold everywhere she looked. She had never been inside a jewelry store as substantial as this one.

"We got your locket from here."

Cammie's eyes widened. "You did?"

He father nodded. "Yes, among many other pieces of jewelry."

I've been wearing a stolen necklace all these years. "I'm not sure how I feel about that."

They walked through the aisles of glass cases. A lady with shoulder-length, brown hair came up to them and asked them if there was a piece of jewelry, she could show them. Her father told her they would let her know.

She nodded and walked up to the next customer a few aisles away.

"I want you to keep wearing that locket without regret, because I know it means a lot to you. I'm going to pay for it."

She looked at him confused. *How can he pay for something that was stolen over twenty-two years ago?*

He walked her over to the gold lockets. When he found a similar locket to hers, he motioned the saleslady over. "I would like to purchase this locket."

The lady wrapped the gold locket up and took him to the cashier.

He took out his wallet and paid cash for the locket. But she was still confused when he had the necklace in his hand and they left the store with it.

"Here's the fun part, Darling. We're going to break in tonight and put this locket back. That should pay for the one you are wearing."

Cammie smiled. "A reverse theft? I'm in." Her father drove them to a luxury hotel and checked them in. Her father told her Simon had slipped some black clothes in her luggage for tonight. *He knew about this all along. Of course he did.*

*****

Cammie held the newly purchased locket in her glove-covered hands. She followed close behind her father into the dark show room. She got that rush she'd had back in Africa. It was bizarre though, breaking in to put something back, rather than steal it. They reached the counter where the locket had been. Her father carefully took out the locket and placed it back in its home.

"There, now your locket has been paid for." She waited

while he expertly turned the alarms back on. They got back in the SUV her father had backed in the far corner of the lot, where the security cameras didn't reach, then took off their gloves and hats.

"I appreciate you doing that for me," Cammie said, holding onto the locket around her neck.

"I would do anything for you, Darling. All I ever wanted was your happiness."

They went back to the hotel to spend the night. She couldn't wait to find out the last place her father wanted to show her.

*****

"I'm glad you asked me to go on this trip with you," Cammie said, as her father parked the SUV at a park.

"So am I. I think it was time for me to show you the things I kept hidden for so long."

"So where are we going now?"

"Geocaching. See, I've already put the coordinates into my GPS. We will follow the GPS within about fifteen feet of the location, then the rest is up to us."

"So what exactly are we looking for?" Cammie followed her father on a dirt trail.

"The container will be the size of a large shoebox."

They walked along the trail through the park, trees surrounding them, until her father stopped.

"Okay, we are close enough to look for the cache."

Cammie looked around them. There were lots of trees and a few shrubs. Her father went up to the trees and looked up. She got down on her knees and looked under the shrubs.

"I don't see anything," she said.

"Keep looking." Her father went over to a cluster of

ferns and looked.

Cammie walked over to some large rocks that were piled in a mound right off the path. There were three large ones and then a flat one on top. She heaved the top rock off and inside saw the container. "I've got it!"

He walked over to her. "Great job. Open it up."

Cammie did as he instructed. Inside was a cherry-lacquer box. She gasped as she lifted her mother's old jewelry box out of the container.

Her father smiled. "She would have wanted you to have it."

"It's beautiful. I love it." She opened the box and ran her fingers over the soft velvet lining.

"There is one more reason I brought you to this park."

Cammie turned to look at him. "Oh?"

"Follow me."

Curious, she followed her father off the path and into the trees, holding the jewelry box close to her heart. He seemed to know right where he was going. They climbed up a hill and on the other side was a small waterfall with dark green moss growing all around it. Tiny, purple wild flowers were growing everywhere in the serene little area.

"It's nice," she told him.

"When you were a toddler, we brought you here. Your mother loved this place." He removed a small urn from his bag. "I have your mother's ashes. Will you help me scatter them over the waterfall?"

"You've had mother's ashes all this time?" Her eyes misted.

"Yes, Darling. I've been waiting for you. It didn't feel right to do this without you."

Cammie bit her lip and nodded. "When we were at the

art museum, I swear I could feel her arms around me."

"I feel her presence a lot. I do not doubt that she is always with us, Darling."

"Goodbye, Elizabeth."

"Goodbye, Mother."

They sat together quietly for a while.

Cammie stood up. "Thank you for waiting for me. I never really had closure." Her father hugged her and they headed back to the trail.

Chapter Thirteen

Simon used his contacts to make sure Cammie's house sold. He called Max to tell him there had been no sign of Kostas or his associates. He wanted to tell Cammie that the father/daughter trip was also to keep her safe, until he could make sure they were all out of danger, but Max made him promise not to say anything. The whole time they were gone, he missed her. Never in a million years did he think a woman could have so much pull over him. Crazy thing was, he didn't even mind.

*****

When they pulled into their garage, Cammie's realtor called to tell her there had been a substantial offer on the house. Perfect, she would take the money from the sale of the house to put into their business. Her heart beat wildly at the thought of seeing Simon again.

As soon as she walked in the door, Simon pulled her into a hug. "Did you have a good time?"

She looked into his eyes. "Yes. I learned a lot about my family and myself."

He put his hands around her face and kissed her deeply. "I'm happy you're back."

"Me too."

Simon took her hand and pulled her upstairs. They sat down on Cammie's bed with their hands intertwined.

"So, do you want to tell me where he took you?"

"I think you already know part of it."

Simon nodded. "Yeah, about that, Max made me

promise not to tell you."

"We went to the art museum that inspired me to start painting, to the jewelry store where my parents had their first heist, which you already knew about that, then we scattered my mother's ashes at a serene place that she loved."

Simon hugged her. "Are you okay?"

She nodded. "Yes. I finally have closure."

"Good. You deserve it." Simon rubbed his thumb over her hand.

She got up from the bed. "You know, the trip to the art museum really inspired me. I truly feel the need to paint," she told him. She walked upstairs to the third floor where her art studio was located.

Simon followed her into the studio. "Really?"

She pulled the curtains closed. "Um-hmm, I know exactly what I want to paint."

"What?"

"You." She smiled.

Simon smirked. "You've already done that, remember?"

"Yes, true, but I only painted your *face*," she said, taking off his shirt. "I want to paint *all* of you."

Simon laughed. "You mean nude."

"Yeah." She gathered her paints and brushes.

"You're serious?"

Cammie nodded.

"Well, who am I to say no to art?" He took off the rest of his clothes. "How do you want me to pose?" He smiled and started dirty dancing. "How about this?"

"Be serious, Simon. This is art. You have to stay still. Just pose however you feel comfortable." She got to work and painted Simon the way she saw him.

"You're not going to show this to anyone are you?"

"No, I won't. Just be still," she commanded.

About twenty minutes later, she smiled satisfied. "Okay you can move. I'm finished."

"Well, I think it's only fair that I get to paint you now."

"You're going to paint me?" She pressed her lips together.

"Take off your clothes please," he said.

She did as he said. When she was completely naked, he took a big glob of paint on his brush and spread it all over her chest.

"Simon!" she yelled and burst out laughing.

"What? I'm painting you nude." He laughed.

They both took globs of paint and attacked each other until they were covered in paint.

"It's a good thing your floors aren't carpeted," Simon said, looking around.

She laughed. "Yeah, it's going to take *you* forever to clean up this mess." She took some paper towels out of her art closet and cleaned herself off the best she could. She got dressed and tiptoed downstairs to take a hot shower.

Simon came into her room. "That was some mess, but it was worth it." He grinned.

"I have to say I have never had that much fun with paint before." She giggled. "Did you find a location for our PI Business while I was gone?"

"I found a few possibilities. If it's okay, I'm going to leave the final decision up to Max."

"Fine with me. So, how long do you think it will take me to learn everything you wanted to teach me?"

"I don't know. If we practice every day, a couple of weeks, maybe."

"Let's start tomorrow."

He touched the tip of her nose. “Okay my little protégé.”

*****

Simon opened his closet door and Cammie followed him inside. He unlocked the armoire on the back wall and opened it. Three guns set on the top shelf. The next shelf held bullets and various things she wasn’t sure of.

“The first thing you need is a gun. This is a Glock 17. It’s the most lightweight and has a safety feature. It was the one you carried before.” He handed her the gun. “It’s your gun now. You need to carry it in case you ever run into trouble. This is an ankle holster. You can wear it or keep the gun in your purse. That’s up to you.”

She pointed at the other guns, “What are those?”

“Those are mine, they’re Glock 22s.”

“And those?” she asked, pointing to the second shelf.

“Drills, supplies. We’ll get to that later. Right now we’re going to a shooting range, so I can teach you how to shoot with accuracy.”

“Can’t I just skip the gun lesson and use my stun gun?” she asked.

“You should know how to properly shoot a gun. I want to make sure you can defend yourself if I’m not with you.”

“Okay, if I have to.” Cammie took the gun from him. It was hard to believe something so small could kill someone, but she knew it could, that was why she didn’t want it. She picked up the complicated-looking ankle holster. “I’ll just use my purse.” She handed the gun back to him.

Simon smirked. “It’s not loaded, you can carry it.”

She sighed. “Fine.” She took it back from him and went

down the hall to get her purple Coach purse. She emptied the unnecessary stuff… an emergency chocolate bar, tea bags, sugar packets and pantyhose, to fit the gun inside.

"It fits." She modeled her new gun holder.

"Good, make room for these." He gave her some bullets. She rolled her eyes, took the bullets from him and put them inside a zippered section. *Does my father have guns? Probably.*

They went down to the garage and got in Simon's Corvette. An hour later, they arrived at the shooting range. Simon showed her how to stand and the correct way hold her gun. The best part was when he had his arms around her to help her aim. Even when she could finally make her target, she didn't enjoy shooting. It was loud. And it hurt her hand and shoulder.

"You have the basics down. We'll come back a few more times to make sure you are more comfortable, okay?"

"Okay. I still think a stun gun is the way to go. This thing just makes me nervous," she said, unloading her gun.

"You'll get used to it."

They drove back home and Simon pulled the Corvette into the garage. The garage door started to close, but the sensor stopped it. Simon looked around and didn't see anything. He pressed the garage door button again, this time it closed. As soon as they were in the house there was a loud crash inside the garage. They exchanged glances. He took out his gun that was always tucked in the waistband of his jeans.

He looked at her with seriousness in his eyes. "Stay here."

She swallowed and nodded.

He opened the door and flipped on the light with his gun drawn.

She bit her lip. Their house was like Fort Knox. Their estate was surrounded by a tall iron fence and security cameras. *How could someone get into the garage?*

Five minutes later Simon walked into the kitchen, smiling, holding a long-haired butterscotch-colored cat. The skinny cat jumped from his arms, ran and hid under the sectional in the living room.

Her eyes widened. “A cat?”

“Yeah. A wild one. He climbed on the shelves and knocked down some boxes.”

She glanced toward the sectional. “And why is he now in our living room?”

Simon shrugged. “He looked hungry. I thought I’d give him some milk.”

Cammie shook her head with her hands on her hips. “If you feed him, he’ll never leave.”

Simon took a Lenox bowl out of the cabinet and opened the fridge. “That’s okay. I’ve always wanted a pet.” He took the bowl of milk into the living room to try and coax the cat out.

She rolled her eyes. “What if he starts pooping in the house and clawing everything?”

“Good point, I’ll go buy a litter box and scratch post.” Simon kissed her quick on the lips and walked out the door. She shook her head and went into the living room. Curious, she bent down to look under the sofa, but the cat wasn’t there. *Great.*

*****

Simon came down the hallway, shaking a container of cat food.

She walked out of her room. “You still haven’t found it?”

“Max said he didn’t mind us having a cat.”

“Us?” *He wants to share a cat with me. This could get serious.*

“Don’t you like our cat, Sweetheart?”

She shrugged. “I don’t know. I’ve never had a pet. I guess.”

“Then help me find him. I have to show him the litter box and feed him.”

They searched the entire house. *No sign of the fur ball.* He was as good at being invisible as Simon was.

She gave up. “Cats are supposed to be smart. Just leave everything out. He’ll find it.”

Simon nodded and put his hands on her hips to pull her close. “You know it was sexy the way you handled your gun today.”

“You think so?” She ran her fingers through his hair.

“I know I said we should sleep in separate rooms, but it’s getting hard to resist knowing you are right down the hall.”

“So maybe you should just sneak into my room after everyone else is asleep.”

“You had me at sneak.” His soft lips brushed her neck.

*****

The top of Cammie’s head felt warm. She opened her eyes and nudged Simon. “I found the cat.”

With his eyes still closed, he rolled over. “You did? Where?”

“On top of my head, on my pillow.” She raised her eyes to the cat.

Simon opened his eyes. "Hey, look at that, he likes you." He laughed.

Careful not to disturb the sleeping cat, she slid off her pillow and onto Simon's chest. "Guess we should name him."

"Hmm." He thought for a minute. "How about Leo?"

Cammie laughed. "He's a cat, not a lion."

The alarm clock went off and the cat jumped up and pounced on it.

Simon smiled. "He thinks he is."

She got up to take a quick shower and decided to go run. She didn't go as much as she used to and wanted to keep in shape. With Simon's eating habits, she would have to do something to be able to keep fastening her jeans. She slipped on her running shorts and put her hair in a ponytail. The house was quiet as she tiptoed downstairs.

The cool morning air woke her up and made her feel alive. She jogged around her father's estate, big enough to circle and still get a decent run in. She loved living with her father, Simon and Nora. They all had ample space of their own, but she took comfort in knowing they all lived under the same roof. She slowed down as she got back to the front door where Nora was stood, looking anxious.

"Dear, I wanted to talk to you."

"Sure."

"I really like Ma– your father. I just wanted to make sure that you were alright with me spending so much time with him."

Cammie nodded. "You've always been like family to me. I'm thrilled you and my father are getting along so well."

"Thank you. You look like you are really happy, too. I don't know if I have ever seen you this happy."

"You noticed?" Cammie laughed.

They went back inside. Nora had hot tea steaming in the tea maker and pancakes stacked a mile high. Simon took half the stack and poured half a bottle of syrup on them. As Cammie ate her third pancake, she was glad she had run this morning.

"Today I'm going to teach you the basics about safes and how to crack them. It would probably take you about a year to master cracking a safe. I can open just about any safe in under fifteen minutes, but I have been doing it for about ten years."

Simon educated her on the many types of safes. He showed her how the inside of the locks worked and explained gates, fences and wheels. He showed her his safe cracking tools and gave her basic instruction on how to use chisels, diamond drill bits and pry bars.

She yawned. "This all sounds really complicated to me."

He smiled and walked back to his armoire and opened a drawer. "Not when you have this." He pulled out some kind of little gadget and plugged it into his laptop. He hooked the other end of the gadget to a safe lock and moved his fingers fast across the keys. The safe opened.

Her eyes widened. "How'd you do that?"

"I kind of took this from a master computer hacker. He stole my diamond collection with this baby. I not only stole my collection back, I took his one of a kind safe opening program. To my knowledge, there's not another one of these out there, unless, he's made another one."

She rolled her eyes. "If you had this magic, safe opener the whole time, why did I have to listen to the history of safe cracking for four hours?"

He smirked. "Because, it's good to know."

She shook her head. "Does my father know about this?"

"Yes," he said.

"You trust him?"

"Yes."

"You trust me?"

"Yes."

"Good," she said.

"Besides we are out the jewel business remember? That was the one sure way I knew your father was out. I told him about it after he told me he was finished. He never tried to take it once. He never even asked to see it. You have no idea how much a jewel thief would want to get their hands on this. You would be unstoppable with it."

"So why did *you* quit then?"

"Your father showed me that there was more to life than jewels. The way he talked about his family. The way he opened up his home to me and got me out of trouble. Sure, I wasn't ever going to fully quit, until I met you. I guess when you finally have something worth losing, everything changes."

She smiled. "Aww, Simon."

"I'm getting hungry, would you like to go out to lunch with me?"

"You mean go grab some fast food through a drive through?" She smirked.

"No, I mean like a real restaurant that you sit down inside and have a nice meal with your girlfriend."

She liked the sound of her being his girlfriend. "Sure, just let me go change. I'm still in shorts."

"Meet me downstairs in thirty minutes."

"Okay."

Cammie ran down the hall to her room. This would be their first official date. She jumped in the shower and washed off as fast as she could. She dried her hair and applied her makeup a little more carefully than usual. She flung open her closet door, scanned the dresses, and decided on a short sexy black one. She slipped on her black heels and a grabbed a black beaded clutch. She checked herself in the mirror one last time, before walking downstairs.

Wearing black slacks, a black shirt and white blazer, Simon stood, looking out the back window. He turned around when he heard her heels on the floor. "You're beautiful."

"You look pretty amazing yourself."

They walked out to his car and he opened her door.

"So where are you taking me?"

"You'll see." Simon drove to a restaurant called The Filet Mignon. He parked the car and opened her door. "It may not be as good as yours, but this is supposed to be the best steak-house in town."

They walked inside the dark restaurant and Simon gave them his last name. They were seated at a private table in the back. There were candles lit at every table giving a romantic vibe. Each table also had a mini-chandelier hung over it with a dim light. Soft music played in the background.

"This place is so nice," Cammie said, looking around.

A waiter brought menus and ice water. She opened her menu to various steaks and pasta dishes. The waiter came back to take their order and she ordered the house specialty, filet mignon. Simon ordered the same and a bottle of red wine.

"This is amazing," she said. The waiter brought their

wine and a basket of bread.

Simon handed her a piece of bread. "Not as amazing as you."

She took a bite and moaned. "That is so good."

"Yours was better," Simon told her.

"I don't know. I think it's a tie."

After they were both stuffed, Simon paid the waiter.

When they walked out of the restaurant, they had to shade their eyes from the bright sun.

"Thanks for lunch."

Simon opened the door for her. "You're welcome."

As Simon drove back home she asked him, "So what do you have planned for me for the rest of the day?"

"I'm going to show you how to disarm an alarm system."

She shook her head. "Do I even need to ask why?"

"You never know when you are going to need the skills I'm teaching you. Someday you'll thank me."

"I wonder if our business is legal, why do I have to learn all these *illegal* skills?"

"Sweetheart, if we're going to be going after criminals we have to think like one. Maybe even, act like one occasionally. Don't worry, after I show you how to bypass an alarm system... I'll show you how to not get caught." He smiled.

Her eyes widened. "What am I getting myself into?"

"Having second thoughts about me being your partner?"

She shook her head. "Not a chance."

Chapter Fourteen

Cammie picked up her mother's jewelry box from the mantel in her bedroom. She was on her way to visit her aunt and wanted to show Eve how beautiful it was. As she walked down the stairs, wildcat whooshed through her legs causing her to drop the jewelry box and grab the stair rail to keep from falling.

The box fell all the way down the stairs and landed on the hard floor.

"Bad Leo. Bad kitty." The cat was already out of sight.

Her heart fell as she looked down to the jewelry box. *Please don't be broken.* She went down the remaining stairs and reached to pick up the box. She sighed when she saw a small crack in the bottom. When she examined the damage closer, she saw something white inside. She opened the jewelry box and pulled on the bottom drawer. When it wouldn't open all the way, she tugged harder, until the drawer came out all the way. Her heart raced when she saw it was a white leather-bound diary. *Mother's diary.*

With a deep breath, she sat down on the stairs and opened to the first entry.

September 1

Dear Diary,

My great-grandmother Clara just told me a story I'm not sure I can believe. She said we have a family heirloom that was stolen from us long ago. She said that with me being the oldest Royce woman, after she's gone, it will be my responsibility to find the heirloom and make sure it is passed along to the next generation. She mumbled something about it being passed along every twenty-two years. Great-grandmother is forgetful lately. Although, she looked at me with such certainty when she told me this story.

Cammie paused to think about what she had just read. She had known that her mother's mother died when she was eighteen, from scarlet fever. That was about all she knew about her grandmother, but she had never heard her mother talk about her great-grandmother. Intrigued, she turned to the next entry.

September 22
Dear Diary,
My great-grandmother took my hands in hers today and made me promise to get the heirloom back. When I asked her what it was. She smiled and said it was the most beautiful thing she had ever laid her eyes on. She called it the Royce Ruby. When I asked her how to find it, she told me about a notorious jewel thief in Greece. He had stolen our ruby. I was to seduce him. I am only nineteen, what do I know of seduction?

Cammie shut the diary. She had a feeling where this was headed. *Can it be? Can the ruby Mother and Father stole before I was born, rightfully have been Mother's all along? Can the man who had Mother murdered be the same man great-great-grandmother told Mother to seduce?* Just to be sure she had read the passages correctly, she reread them again. She closed the diary. *Holy crap!*

Simon came downstairs and she shoved the diary into

her purse, then picked up the jewelry box.

"Everything okay?"

"Yeah." She gave him a quick kiss. "I'm on my way to see Eve."

*****

After she took the elevator up to see her aunt, she nervously knocked on Eve's door. She'd left the jewelry box in her car.

Eve opened her door and smiled. "Come in. How are you?"

"Great." Cammie looked around her suite decorated in lime-green and pink. A big white furry rug sat in the middle of the living room. On top of it was a bright pink fabric colored sofa and two pale-pink acrylic chairs. The walls and throw pillows were lime- green. There was an oversized white chandelier that hung over the arrangement. *Definitely a woman's décor.* "I like what you have done with the place."

"Thanks, it looks a lot like my old apartment, only bigger."

"Cool colors."

"They are bold, but I think they work. Did I ever tell you that I used to be a designer?"

"No. Why did you stop?"

"I got my job with the magazine when they did an article about one of my rooms. The editor was so impressed with my style she wanted me to come and help her edit the pictures to be used for The Modern Home Magazine."

"Wow."

"Yeah, I miss decorating sometimes, but my job pays really well and I like the people I work with."

"That's great."

"Well, come in and sit down, can I get you some tea or a soda?"

"Tea would be good." Cammie sat down on the pink sofa and Eve brought her some tea.

Eve sat down beside her. "How are things with Simon?"

"Wonderful. He makes me really happy. How about you? Anyone special in your life?"

"No. I'm much too busy with my career to worry about a man."

"Aunt Eve, you can have both." Cammie paused. She wasn't sure how to bring her question up without telling her about the diary. "What can you tell me about Clara Royce?"

Eve's eyes widened and her face turned pale. "How do you know about Clara?"

Cammie bit her lip. "I can't really say right now. Can you just tell me about her? Anything at all?"

"Can I get you some cookies?" Eve said, standing up and heading toward the kitchen.

Cammie sighed. "Sure." Eve was stalling. *Why?*

Eve came back in the living room carrying a plate of sugar cookies.

"Thanks," Cammie said, taking one. "Now about Clara?"

Eve blew a stray curl out of her eyes. "I don't know a lot about her. Our mother died when I was sixteen. Your mother and I moved in with our eccentric great-grandmother after the funeral. I was shy and your mother was outgoing. She was older so she did her own thing and I stayed in my room most of the time to read and study." Eve looked down at her lap.

Cammie nodded, waiting for her to continue.

"Great-grandmother never really took an interest in me like she did your mother. I went into my shell when our mother died. I suppose until now, I never let myself get fully attached to another person."

Sounds familiar.

"I always suspected that for some reason it was great-grandmother's fault that Elizabeth became a jewel-thief." Eve smiled. "I know that's ridiculous."

It wasn't, but she would read the entire diary before she told her aunt.

Eve tilted her head. "Did your mother talk about our great Grandmother much?"

Cammie shook her head. "Not much. I'd better go."

"Oh, okay, come back when you have more time."

"I will, I promise. I'm working on something with my father and Simon right now."

Eve's eyebrows shot up.

"Completely legal. We're going to start a business together."

"A business? You, your father and Simon?"

"Yes. A PI business. We have a lot of details to work out, but we are all excited about it."

Eve shook her head. "Too much like your mother. Just promise me you will be careful. I just got you back."

Cammie made an X over her heart. "Cross my heart."

Eve gave her a hug. "Come back anytime. I mostly work from home so I am usually here."

"I will. Bye Eve."

*****

Cammie called Simon and asked him to meet her at Ice

Creamery a few streets over from The Kipton. She not only loved the hand-scooped ice cream, but the charm of the place as well. She arrived at the building with a black and white polka dot awning over the door. A white wicker bench sat out front. She went inside where there were about a dozen round metal tables, no bigger around than a large dinner plate.

She took a seat to wait for Simon and opened her mother's dairy to read the next entry.

October 1

Dear Diary,

I have done my research on the Royce Ruby. It was, in fact, stolen by a notorious jewel thief in Greece. His name is Kostas Avramidis. He is old enough to be my father. I must find another way. Great-grandmother is getting weaker. I feel a heavy burden has been placed upon my shoulders. The worst part is when she is gone, I will be all alone in this secret quest.

She paused. The secrets were so much deeper than she ever realized. *Did Eve ever find out? Does Father know? Was the ruby I retrieved the genuine Royce Ruby?* The diary was bringing up a lot of questions. She continued to read hoping for answers.

December 2

Dear Diary,

RIP Great-grandmother Clara. Know that I will do everything I promised. The Royce Ruby will be back where it belongs one day. I think I have found a way. I met a jewel thief today. His name is

Max Adams. He will teach me all I need to know. He is also the most handsome man I've ever seen. It will be hard not to fall in love with him. But I am focused. I know what must be done. Forgive me Max.

She gasped. *Mother, what did you do?*

The parlor door opened and Simon walked in.

Simon ordered them both an ice cream cone and sat down with her.

"Thanks." She lifted the diary up for him to see. "Leo made me drop my mother's jewelry box down the stairs this morning. I found this diary hidden inside."

Simon raised an eyebrow. "Anything interesting?"

Cammie put the diary back into her purse. "More secrets. When I met you, I thought all the secrets my family kept were revealed." She paused. "I was wrong."

Simon studied her face. "You going to tell me about the secrets?"

"Later, I'm still trying to process it myself." She put the last bite of cone in her mouth and chewed.

*****

Simon scratched Leo's head as he purred. He couldn't stop thinking about Cammie's mother's diary. She had been distracted and secretive, which was so unlike her. As much as he wanted to sneak a peek, Cammie had a right to her privacy. Which he'd already violated too many times to count. So he'd be patient and hope that she would tell him what was bothering her more sooner than later.

*****

Cammie couldn't get comfortable. She tried to fall asleep but her mother's diary was calling to her. She looked over at Simon, already asleep. She got out of bed, grabbed the dairy and headed into the bathroom. She drew herself a hot bubble bath and placed the diary on her teak reading tray. Once submerged into the hot, soapy water she opened the diary and began to read.

January 19

Dear Diary,

I had my first heist. With Max's help, I stole a pearl necklace. Max is a great teacher. I am preparing for the day he will help me get the Royce Ruby. I am starting to have feelings for him. I want to tell him the truth but I fear I cannot. I have a plan. Maybe somehow I can have Max and the ruby.

She added some more hot water to the tub and continued to read.

July 25

Dear Diary,

My plan is in motion. I married Max. He is wonderful. I believe our love is fate. If not for the ruby, I would never have crossed paths with him. I am pregnant with a daughter. Fate again. After we steal the ruby for our unborn child, we will have a normal life together. I know a way to keep the Royce Ruby safe for twenty-two years. Max, our child and I will be a family. I want to tell him everything. When our child is twenty-two, I will explain what I had to do. I pray they can both understand.

She looked up and stared out into the bathroom. *How can I feel betrayal and pride for Mother at the same time?* Her very existence was part of a calculated plan to keep a ruby safe and trap her father. Yet, her mother was smart and brave. Her mother did give her the best childhood any girl could ask for up until she was fifteen. She blinked the tears out of her eyes and continued to the last entry.

May 12

Dear Diary,
I am happy. Max is the best husband. Cammie is a wonderful daughter. Kostas is after the Royce Ruby. He has never stopped looking for it. I have another plan. It isn't about keeping the ruby safe any longer. I have to keep my darling, Cammie protected. I will not give my fifteen year old daughter, the burden that was once placed on my shoulders. If Max and I disappear until Cammie is twenty-two, she will have a chance to have her own dreams come true. If something happens to me, I will leave it up to fate once again to decide if my story is told or I take it with me to my grave. This will be my last entry. May the Royce Ruby end up where it is destined to be. The information I have obtained and a map to the Avramidis Mansion is written inside the back of this diary.

She shook with sobs, then calmness came over her. In that single moment everything seemed as clear to her as it must have to her mother all those years ago. She knew what must be done. She would tell Simon she needed a short vacation alone, then she would take a commercial flight to Greece.

*****

In the garage, Simon stood behind Cammie and put his hand on her shoulder. "So what if I grabbed you from behind?"

Cammie grabbed his arm with one hand, twisted and reached to hit him with the other. He grabbed her hand as it was about to strike his face.

"Good job."

"Thanks."

"Now what if I had a knife from behind held against your neck?" He stood behind her with a screwdriver used as makeshift knife.

"I grab your hand and push it away from me." She took a hold of his wrist and pushed it out in front of her. "Then I turn and kick you." She did the motion slowly as she explained. He caught her foot and sat it back down.

He smiled. "You're catching on."

She nodded, tired and out of breath.

They'd been doing the self-defense lessons for the past two hours.

"Okay. I'll do a random attack and we'll see how you react. Pretend I'm a big ugly assailant." He came up to her and lightly grabbed the top of her hair with his fist.

Without thinking, she took her fist and hit his knuckles into her head, then kicked him in the shin.

He grabbed a hold of his leg. "Shit, that hurt." He pulled up his sweats to look at where she'd kicked him.

She bit her lip. "Oh, I'm so sorry. I didn't mean to really kick you. I'll go get you some ice."

He nodded and sat down.

She put her hand over her mouth and went inside. She got a baggie out and filled it with ice. Her father was drinking some tea and reading the paper with Leo curled up on his lap.

"How's it going out there? Are you okay?" he asked, looking up.

She held up the bag of ice. "This is for Simon." She grimaced. "I kicked him by accident."

He chuckled. "And here I was worried about you."

She went back into the garage. "Here, I'm sorry." She placed the ice on the lump that had come up on his shin.

"That's okay. I think I taught you too well. So well, in fact, I have nothing else to teach you."

"So did you talk to my father about the name I thought of?"

"Yes and he said that he wanted you to choose the name, so I guess we'll call our agency Case Solved."

"I hope we can live up to our name," she joked.

"We will. I think the three of us will make a good team." He handed her a stun gun. "Here's your stun gun as promised. It's up to you now which gun you want to carry."

She took the stun gun and smiled. "I promise if things ever get bad enough, I'll carry the Glock."

"We better get ready. Max wants to show us the place he got for the agency. He said it's really close."

They went downstairs and into the garage where her father was waiting in the agency's new dark blue SUV. The windows were tinted and bulletproofed. A father cannot be too careful when his only daughter is hunting criminals, he'd told her when he bought it for their business.

Her father drove, Simon rode shotgun and Cammie sat

behind her father. About ten minutes later, he turned right on Sterling. Where an old travel agency used to sit, was now a renovated, tumbled-brick building with a newly paved parking lot. Her father pulled right up to the door. Etched in the glass of the door was Case Solved.

"I love it." Cammie beamed.

"Looks great," Simon said.

"This is where I'll be spending my days. I wanted to be comfortable," her father explained. He unlocked the door and then disarmed the state of the art alarm system. They followed him inside.

"Wow!" Cammie said, as she looked around. Five modern looking chairs with metal legs and leather seats lined the wall. There was a huge mahogany desk with a leather chair behind it in the middle of the room. A laptop, phone and calendar were on top of the desk. A leather bench was in front of the desk for clients to sit on. There was a large globe on a wooden stand next to the desk. A wooden file cabinet sat on the back wall. The walls were wallpapered with antique looking maps. In the center of the room, a huge area rug covered the polished cement floors.

Her father led them to the back that opened to a bathroom and mini-kitchen.

"This place is great," Simon told him.

Her father laughed. "I had a little help. I talked Eve into decorating for us. I've put the word out to some of my contacts. It shouldn't be long until we get our first client."

Cammie smiled. "It may have to wait a week. I want to do one more thing before we take our first case."

"What?" her father and Simon asked, in unison.

Cammie wasn't a good liar, but she'd have to be

convincing if this were to work. "So much has happened. I need to get away by myself. I'm going to London to immerse myself in art for a week. My flight leaves in a few hours." While an art trip sounded awesome, London wasn't where she was really headed. She hated keeping this from them, but she had to.

Her father nodded. "Take all the time you need, but at least let Nate fly you."

She knew if she were to keep this a secret, she couldn't take her father's jet. "I already paid for my flight. I want to do this my way." The Royce Ruby belonged to her family, to future generations. Her mother died trying to do the right thing. She would not let it have been for nothing.

*****

Simon drove her to the airport. "I'd love to know what's going through that pretty head of yours."

She looked away, afraid he'd be able to read her. "Nothing, just going to miss you."

He pulled the car up to drop her off at the gate. "Are you leaving because of something I did or didn't do?"

She hugged him tight. "No. It's me. I won't be long, maybe a week, tops."

Simon's hazel eyes stared down into hers. "Does this have anything to do with the diary you've been reading?"

Damn he's good. "It's about me, Simon. Something I must do, for me." She would avoid the truth as much as possible. "You can handle not seeing me for a week, right?"

Simon handed her the luggage and shut the trunk. "Go be inspired. See you next week." He kissed her quick on the lips. She knew he was upset.

She got onto the plane with her mother's diary inside her carry-on. As the plane took off, she looked out the window. *What am I doing? What if I get killed the way Mother did?* She bit her lip. Her stomach sickened.

She had once held that ruby in her hands and felt despise for it. Were things so different now? She looked down at her carry-on. As much as she wished they weren't, things were different. She took out her mother's diary and reread every passage to reaffirm what she was doing. Still she couldn't shake that uneasy feeling.

Chapter Fifteen

Simon slammed the door to his Corvette and stomped inside. He was glad no one was home to see his temper tantrum. *She was lying. Miss I-hate-secrets herself.* And he had a feeling it had to do with that damn diary. Now he wished he would have read it. If he followed her and she found out he might lose her. On the other hand if he did nothing and something happened to her, he'd never forgive himself and Max would kill him.

He punched the pillow on his bed in frustration and Leo ran out from under the bed. He rubbed his face. He had no choice. He had to let her go. She'd be back.

*****

Once Cammie was checked into her meager hotel suite, under a fake name of course, she didn't waste any time. She put on her big floppy hat and sunglasses to blend in with the crowd. She grabbed a taxi to the opposite end of town in the vicinity of Kostas Avramidis' mansion.

Armed with her smart phone translator, she paid the taxi driver and stepped out onto the stone walk. Kostas' neoclassical mansion stood at the top of the hill about five hundred steps up. The peach color of the building contrasted highly with the white of the six enormous columns. Huge ferns lined the steps. *That bastard has my family's ruby somewhere up in that massive house of his.*

The town square at the bottom of the hill where she

stood was alive with activity. People meandered along the street shops. Women and children rode bicycles with baskets full of bread. Stray cats and dogs walked the streets looking for food or a home, a few people stopped to feed them a bite of food.

Cammie decided to walk a block down the narrow street to a café or taverna as the Greeks called it. The bright yellow umbrellas provided a canopy of shade from the blazing sun. She had a clear view of the mansion from her table on the sidewalk. She wished she had some brilliant plan on how to get the ruby back. Unfortunately, she didn't. She bit her lip as she looked up at the mansion.

A waiter walked up to her table. She was able to translate her English to Greek well enough to order dinner. She ate her spinach pie and fresh baked bread. After her Mediterranean meal, she walked along the brick-paved street gazing up at the mansion. People on their laptops and cell phones were an awkward mix with the ancient domed mosques and age-old crumbling buildings.

An idea struck her. She tucked her hair up under her hat, pulled her hat further down over her face and took out her camera. She walked toward the steps up to the mansion and snapped a few pictures. She walked halfway up the steps before she was stopped by a bodyguard. She played dumb.

"I'm sorry. I got carried away taking pictures of this beautiful place." She smiled hoping he would buy her confused tourist act. The tan muscular guy nodded and motioned for her to go the other way. She did so without turning back. *Damn, the place is secure.* She knew it would be. *How will I ever get inside?* She spent the rest of the day trying to figure that out.

*****

After her shower, Cammie went down to the hotel dining room to eat a quick breakfast of creamy yogurt and delicious bread. Greeks knew how to make bread. Dressed in a yellow floral sundress she'd bought from a shop last night, she headed outside to grab a taxi back to the town square.

She spent her morning watching the Avramidis estate and didn't see anyone coming or going from the mansion. Tired of walking and hungry, she sat down on one of the many wicker sofas inside a café. As she was eating her gyro, a woman in her late forties, wearing a long dress came up and sat down in front of her.

The brown-eyed lady smiled. "Are you American?" Until Cammie heard her speak, she had thought her to be Greek.

"Yes and you?" Cammie asked.

She nodded. "Mmm, I'm Lydia. Originally from Ohio." She held out her hand.

Cammie shook her hand. "Cammie from California."

"Beautiful mansion," Lydia said, nodding to the Avramidis mansion.

"Yes, it's lovely." Cammie smiled.

They smiled and eyed each other. Lydia had long silky brown hair. Her tan skin was flawless and her posture showed confidence. She guessed her occupation to be modeling.

"I've seen you watching the mansion all day. What is your interest in Kostas?" Lydia asked.

Cammie felt her face burn. "Who's Kostas?"

Lydia looked up at the mansion when she spoke. "He's a monster. He is very powerful. And my ex-husband."

Cammie tried to stay calm. "Your ex-husband?" She treaded carefully. "He must not be a *total* monster if you loved him once."

Lydia laughed. "Loved him, no. Never. I wish him dead."

"Why are you telling me this?" Cammie asked.

Lydia smiled. "Because for the first time since I have been here, in the last ten years, I saw you look up at the mansion with the same despise I have for it. You know exactly who my ex-husband is. Now why don't you tell me what he's done to you, to make you hate him as much I do?"

Cammie felt like she could trust her but she had to be sure. Too much was at stake. "You first. Why do you hate him?"

Lydia's eyes glazed over as if she were in a trance. "Ten years ago, I came here for vacation before I went off to college. I had always wanted to come to Greece. I met Kostas. Even though he was older, his looks made up for his age. He was looking for a wife. I was looking for a love affair. He knew just what to say to a naive American girl to make her fall hard and fast. He promised a life of luxury, power and passion."

She saw tears in Lydia's eyes as she stopped to take a drink of her wine.

"We were married within two weeks of meeting. As soon as I became Mrs. Avramidis, Kostas changed. He was cold and cruel. He treated me like one of his many possessions." Lydia closed her eyes.

"I'm sorry. That sounds horrible."

Lydia opened her eyes. "Yes. Horrible. After five miscarriages, he found me unfit to be his wife. I think that it was a blessing I was unable to carry his child. He let me go, with nothing." She took a deep breath. "I am too broke and too ashamed to go back home."

"I'm sorry. Has he remarried?"

"No. We've only been divorced for a month."

Cammie sat down her wine. "You're right. I do hate Kostas but maybe not as much as you."

"But you're here for a reason. I can see it in your eyes. Maybe we can help each other. I want Kostas to pay for what he did to me."

Cammie still wasn't sure if she should trust her. She did have a point though. If they worked together, it could benefit them both. "What did you have in mind?"

"It would help if I knew what you wanted. Why are you here?"

Cammie pressed her lips together. "He has something that belonged to my mother. Something that means a lot to my family, I'm here to get it back."

Lydia nodded. "He stole jewelry from you, right?" She continued when Cammie didn't answer. "I know he's a jewel thief. I also know where he keeps his stash. I can help you."

Cammie hesitated. "What will you get from helping me?"

"Revenge. And I need money to go back home and restart my life. He tricked me. I should own half of his fortune."

"Do you have a plan?"

Lydia smiled. "Does that mean we are going to help each other?"

Cammie nodded. "Yes. I guess it does."

*****

Lydia's hotel was closer to the Avramidis mansion. The peeling plaster with layers of aged paints in teals, yellows and blues, to Cammie's artistic eye, was beautiful. Lydia's small bedroom window had a perfect view of the mansion and the sea beyond.

"I'm glad you came here, Cammie. I've been so lonely. While the Greek people are friendly, they're also frightened of my ex-husband and will not talk ill of him. I've been alone with my hate for a very long time."

"I'm glad too. I hope we can both get what we want."

Cammie's phone vibrated in her purse, she saw it was Dinah was calling.

"Hello," Cammie answered. She heard sobbing. "Dinah, what is it?"

"Keith... he's been ssshot."

"Oh my God. Where is he?"

"He's...He's in the ICU at." Dinah paused to blow her nose. "At Community Hospital."

"I'll get on the next flight home. Hang in there." Cammie hung up her phone and looked at Lydia. "My best friend's husband was shot. He's in the ICU. I have to go."

Lydia frowned and nodded. "I understand."

Cammie's eyes widened and took Lydia's hand. "I'll be back. I promise. We'll get Kostas." Cammie wrote down her cell number. "If you can wait, I'll help you."

"I'll wait. I've waited this long, right?"

Without hesitation, Cammie grabbed her suitcase and headed to the airport.

*****

It had been an exhausting flight home. Cammie was

worried sick about Keith and Dinah. As she walked down the stark white hall of Community Hospital the smell of disinfectant and antiseptic stung her nose. Her heart ached for Dinah. *Please let Keith be okay.* She walked up to the desk and the receptionist pointed her in Dinah's direction. Dinah turned when Cammie came up behind her. Cammie hugged her and looked at her reddened, tear-streaked face.

"Thank you for coming. They got the bullet out yesterday. He lost a lot of blood."

Cammie held Dinah's hand. "What's the doctor saying?"

Dinah took a deep breath. "He says he did all he could, that it's up to Keith now." She rubbed her dry lips together. Cammie reached into her purse and handed her some lip-gloss.

"Thanks. I must look a mess." Dinah applied the lip-gloss and handed it back to her.

"You look great for what you've been through."

"My parents have the kids. Your father and Nora were here yesterday. Simon is actually here now. He went down to the cafeteria to get me some coffee."

Cammie smiled. *Simon is here.* She had only been gone for a few days, but missed him like crazy. "I wish I could've gotten here sooner."

"Well, it's not like London is close."

"No." Cammie hated lying to her friend and her family. She would have to lie again when she went back to Greece.

Simon walked up to them. He handed Dinah a paper cup of coffee. He put his arms around Cammie. She let him embrace her. He whispered, "I missed you."

She kept her head close to him letting his spicy-cinnamon-citrus cologne drown out the sickening smell of the ICU. "I missed you so much."

The doctor came out of Keith's room and looked at Dinah. "He's asking for you."

Dinah smiled. "He's awake?" The doctor nodded. She followed him into the room. Cammie walked over to the lounge with Simon and sat down. "What happened? How'd he get shot?"

Simon ran his fingers through his wavy hair. "He was off duty, visiting a buddy down south. He tried to stop a bar fight and the guy pulled out a gun and shot him. The bullet nicked his heart. He's lucky to be alive."

"Do you think he'll be okay?"

"Yeah. Keith is a tough guy. He'll pull through."

"Thank God. Thanks for being here for Dinah."

Simon smiled. "No problem. Sorry your trip got cut short. Well, no actually I'm not," he teased.

"How's my father?"

"He's great. He's at home with Nora."

"I can't wait to see them. How about Leo?"

Before he could answer, Dinah walked up to them.

"How is he?" Cammie asked.

"He's asking for a cheeseburger and a beer." She laughed.

Cammie smiled. "That's a good sign."

"The doctor wants me to let him rest. Can you drive me home so I can get a shower and change my clothes?"

Simon and Cammie stood up. "Of course. Let's go. You should eat something, too."

Dinah nodded. "I hate to leave him." She looked back toward his room and bit her lip.

"I'll stay," Simon told her. He handed Cammie the keys to his Corvette. "Cammie can take you."

Dinah looked relieved. “Thanks that’ll be great. I’ll be quick.”

Simon sat back down. “Take your time.”

Cammie hugged him. “Be back soon.”

“We have a lot to talk about when you get back. For now, go take care of your friend.”

*****

“They’re releasing him today.” Dinah was almost giddy.

Cammie smiled. “That’s wonderful.” They were standing with Dinah inside Keith’s room. He had been moved from the ICU and was looking much better.

Keith sat up in his bed. “I appreciate everything you two have done. It’s good to know we have such good friends.”

“You’d have done the same for us,” Simon told him.

Cammie smiled. “We’re so glad you’re okay.”

Keith shook his head. “I always knew being a cop, there was a chance I’d get shot someday. Never once did I think I’d get shot off duty.”

Dinah looked at him, hands on her hips. “Next time you break up a fight, you better be wearing a vest. I am too young to be a widow.”

“You got it, babe. Now get me out of here so I can have a beer.”

Dinah smiled. “After what you put me through, I need a few.”

Simon and Cammie laughed.

*****

Simon kept his eyes on the road and asked, “Did you

have a chance to paint?"

"Not really. I was inspired though." *Not a lie, just not the full truth.*

"Sweetheart, I've been patient. I'm not an idiot. You were reading your mother's diary nonstop, then all of a sudden you wanted to go off to London by yourself in the middle of a case, for art, on a commercial plane?"

Cammie bit her lip and sighed. "I know you're not an idiot. You're too smart for *my* own good." She let out a little laugh. "If I tell you, you have to promise not to try to stop me. I call the shots." She looked into his eyes searching for agreement.

"I thought we were a team," Simon finally said.

"We are. Come on," Cammie said, standing up and slipping on her sandals. Simon followed her to her art studio. She reached behind a stack of canvases and pulled out her mother's diary. She handed it to Simon. "Go ahead read it. Then maybe you'll understand."

He walked down the hall to her bedroom. He sprawled out on the suede sofa and opened the diary. As he read, she watched for his expression to change, but it didn't. She couldn't take it anymore. His jaw was tight. She didn't want to tell him, but she didn't want to lie to him either.

He handed her the diary. "Tell me you didn't go to Greece. Tell me you wouldn't do anything that stupid, Cammie."

Uh-oh, he never calls me Cammie. "Umm, I can't do that." She gulped. "I told you not to talk me out of what I have to do."

He shook his head. "I understand what you want to do. I don't understand why you thought you needed to do it alone."

She stood up and wrapped her arms around him. “Because if anything went wrong, my father would at least have you.”

“You don’t get to make a choice that affects me like that. I decide.” He pulled her tighter to his chest. “What needs to be done, we do it together. We’ll figure it out. Agreed?”

A tear slid down Cammie’s cheek. “Agreed.”

He wiped her cheek and kissed her.

Chapter Sixteen

It took Cammie's eyes a minute to adjust to the darkness when they walked into the tavern. She went to a small, round bar table in the corner and perched herself on a tall stool. Simon left to get their drinks. They had beaten the evening crowd, so the place was near empty.

Cammie traced a finger along the grain of the polished oak table. A small wooden bowl in the center of the table held nuts and she took a few. They didn't frequent places like this, neither of them drank much. They enjoyed some mixed drinks and wine on occasion, but sweet tea was the drink she favored above all else.

Simon came back to the table, a glass in each hand. He sat her drink down in front of her, then took a seat across from her. He pulled up the stool to the table and propped his feet on the footrest.

She took a sip of her smooth, tropical drink.

Simon downed his, then nodded. "Okay, I'm ready."

She blew out a breath. "I stayed in a small hotel, under a fake name, on the opposite side of town from Kostas' mansion. I spent my days going across town watching the mansion. I wore a disguise and didn't get too close." She left out the part about trying to go up the stairs and being stopped by a bodyguard. "The last day I was there, I met Lydia, an American from Ohio. She hates Kostas even more than I do. We were going to work together, before I got the call from Dinah."

Simon looked at her. "How does Lydia know Kostas?"

Cammie bit her lip. "She's his ex-wife."

Simon took her almost untouched drink and finished it off.

*****

He had taken the news better than expected with the help of a little something to take the edge off.

"Promise me you won't go back alone."

Cammie nodded. "I promise."

He pulled a piece of paper out of his pocket. "I guess Lydia is who she said she is."

Cammie skimmed over the paper. "You ran a background check on her?"

"You don't go up against someone like Kostas Avramidis without doing your homework."

"I knew she was telling the truth." She handed him back the papers.

Her cell vibrated in her pocket. She looked over at Simon. "It's Lydia."

"Put her on speaker."

Cammie did as he said and answered.

"We have a window of opportunity. How soon can you get here?"

She looked at Simon. "What kind of window? What's going on?"

"Kostas takes a yearly trip to Croatia. He goes to visit his brother the exact same date every year. I remember because it was the happiest time of my marriage when he was gone."

"Wow, that's awful."

"I know. We may not get another opportunity like this for a long time. The house will still be guarded, but I know a way in and the best time to get past the guards.

Are you in?"

"I'm in. I'll be on the next flight." Cammie disconnected.

"I'll call the pilot. Go ahead and pack."

"Okay."

"Are you going to tell your father about the diary?"

"When we have the ruby back, yes. After that, I don't want any more secrets."

*****

After quick introductions Simon, Cammie and Lydia were getting into the gear he had brought. Head to toe in black, Simon and Cammie followed Lydia through the dark allies of Greece.

"It's this way," Lydia whispered as they cornered the bottom of a hill.

How did my life go from no excitement to heart-pounding excursions? Cammie wasn't afraid, Simon was with her. They all had something to gain from robbing Kostas.

"We are just in time. The guards take a break at 3 a.m. rarely do they have anyone cover for them," Lydia told them.

They stood outside the back employee entrance to the Kostas mansion. Lydia had stolen a key before she left.

Simon withdrew his gun. "I'll go in first to make sure it's clear."

Cammie and Lydia nodded as he took Lydia's key and tried to unlock the door.

"The locks must have been changed." He smiled. "Not a problem."

Lydia looked over at Cammie and she shrugged. She knew how much Simon loved practicing his old skills. He had the door open in under a minute and disappeared inside.

Cammie held her breath until he came back out and motioned them in. Just as Lydia had thought, the guards must have been on break.

Lydia turned to them. "Follow me."

They followed her through the dimly lit halls. After going down a small set of steps, they got to another locked door. Simon performed his magic and got them inside.

The room looked like a blown up version of Simon's jewel room. Millions of dollars of jewels sat on display. Lydia disappeared.

"Where'd she go?" Simon asked.

"I don't know." Cammie looked around frantically. "I don't see the ruby."

"It's here somewhere."

Cammie spotted a painting on the wall that looked like a portrait of her mother. She walked over to the painting and removed it from the wall revealing a small niche holding the Royce Ruby.

"I've got it," Cammie tucked the ruby inside her bra.

Gun shots echoed through the mansion.

Simon grabbed Cammie's hand. "Let's get out of here!"

"But what about Lydia?"

Simon pulled her toward the door. "Your safety is all I care about."

Lydia came running toward them covered in blood. "Run, go!"

Simon pulled Cammie back through the halls and they ran outside.

Once they were a block away, Cammie turned to Lydia, "Are you hurt?"

"No, just go. Take your jewelry and leave."
They all kept running until they got back to the hotel.
"Lydia, whose blood is that?" Cammie had a feeling she already knew the answer.
"My ex-husband will not hurt anyone ever again."
Cammie's mouth dropped open. "I thought he was in Croatia."
Lydia shook her head. "I couldn't tell you what I planned to do."
Simon grabbed their suitcase. "Lydia, you're on your own. Murder wasn't part of the plan."
Cammie followed Simon into the night in a state of shock. Only later on the jet, would she look at the ruby and feel relief.

*****

The mug of tea warmed Cammie's hands as she told her father the story of how she found her mother's diary. Also how she'd gotten back the ruby that started everything. Leo sat on the sofa looking at her intently with his amber eyes as if he were listening to the story as well.
Her father sat with tears in his eyes until she was finished, then he stood up and hugged her close. "Family pact. No more secrets."
Cammie smiled. "No more secrets."
"Darling, when I asked you to move in and go on that trip with me, I wasn't totally honest. I had to keep you safe."
Her head couldn't handle any more. All that mattered was that they were all safe now. "It's okay. I understand."

Her father nodded and looked over at Simon who sat by Cammie's side. "Simon, old friend, thank you for keeping my daughter safe."

Simon stood up to shake her father's hand. "Always."

Cammie finished her tea and went upstairs. The ruby was home, finally. Simon came up behind her and unbuttoned her jeans. She pulled her top over her head as he slowly worked his way up her body with his lips. Once he'd kissed every inch of her naked body, he lifted her up and carried her over to the bed. She arched her body up into his. He smiled and she grabbed a hold of his muscles and pulled him deeper into her.

After they were both out of breath she whispered into Simon's ear, "No more secrets," before she rolled over and fell asleep.

*****

Simon tossed and turned all night, he had to tell her about his past. All the secrets her family had kept from her were out now. He didn't want to be the person keeping anything from her and he never wanted to see that pain on her face again. *But what if she learns who I am and is ashamed of me?* Now he was having second thoughts. As much as he tried to leave his past behind him, somehow it always came back.

He put his arms around her. "I'm ready to tell you about my past."

Cammie kissed him. "Whatever it is, you can trust me."

"It's not that I don't trust you." He looked into her eyes for a moment. "I'm not proud of it that's all."

She held his hand. "My parents weren't Saints, Simon."

He looked away. "No, but at least they always loved

you."

She frowned. Her heart ached for him.

He sighed and stood up. "Go pack. We're taking a road trip."

Before he could change his mind, she ran to her room to pack.

When she came back downstairs, Simon was sitting with Leo on his lap.

She sat down her bag. "When we get back, I think we should open the doors to our PI agency. Would that be okay?"

Simon put Leo down on the sofa and stood up. "I'm ready if you are."

Cammie tilted her head to kiss him. "I'm so ready." She gave Leo a pat on the head. "Okay partner, let's go so we can get back home and open for business with all our secrets behind us."

Simon nodded and took her bag.

*****

All Cammie knew was, they were headed to Canada. Simon said he would tell her the rest when they got to wherever it was they were going.

"So were you born in Canada?" she asked, confused.

"Yes."

She smiled. "Wow, I didn't even know I was dating a Canadian."

Simon laughed.

"Are you a US citizen now?" she asked.

"Yes and that is the last info you're getting from me until we get there." He smiled, slightly.

She sighed. "Fine."

Simon was too quiet. They had been driving since last night.

"We'll sleep here overnight." He pulled his Corvette into a hotel parking lot. She happened to notice he gave the check-in lady false names and paid cash for their room. *Why? Is someone looking for him?* They took the elevator up to the forth floor. They walked in and she smiled. The hotel was as nice as The Kipton. *Good, I can take a bubble bath and order room service.*

Cammie woke up feeling rested. And anxious. Soon she would know things about Simon that he'd kept private for so long. They checked out of the hotel and got in the SUV. Simon turned right at the light to get back on the highway.

"We aren't far. About two more hours," Simon told her.

Where are we going? His past can't be that bad, can it? Maybe I'm going to meet his parents. Maybe he has an ex-wife or crazy ex-girlfriend hiding out somewhere. What if he has an even bigger secret than being a jewel thief?

A couple of hours later, she looked up. They were in the suburbs. Modest brick houses with lots of pine trees. *This is what he is hiding? It doesn't look bad.* He pulled up to a red brick house on the corner and parked the Corvette in front of it.

He turned off the car. "This is where I used to live." He nodded to the house in front of them. "I lived here with my father, Scott and my mother, Lucy."

"Are they in there now?" she asked.

"No. I'm not sure who lives there now."

They sat in the Corvette looking at the house in front of them on Whistle Lane. It was plain and boxed shaped. No shutters. There was a gray metal storm door over the white front door. A couple of pine trees stood on either side of the house. The yard was mowed, but there weren't any flowers planted. A sidewalk stretched from the street up to the door.

"My father was an alcoholic. We didn't see him all that much, but he did work enough to pay the bills. Beer was the alcohol of his choice."

Cammie frowned. "Is that why you don't like beer?"

"Probably. So when I was eight he decided he loved beer more than my mother and me and took off."

She shook her head. "Jerk."

"Yeah, my thoughts exactly. He left us with no money. My mother had never worked. We lost the house."

She felt her eyes watering and tried to hold the tears in. She wanted him to finish his story. Simon got out of the Corvette, reached under the seat and pulled out a small hand-held shovel.

She looked at him. "What's that for?"

"Before we left our house, I buried something in the backyard. I told myself I would come back to get it one day."

She stood there and looked at him. He was going to go digging in someone's yard. She looked around to see if anyone was outside.

"Are you coming?" he asked.

"Absolutely." She followed him back, hoping the owner of the house wasn't home or didn't own a shotgun.

The curtains were drawn. No lights on. *Good, it doesn't look like anyone is home.* They walked to a small storage shed in the back of the yard and went behind it. Simon stood in the middle of the back of the shed. He counted five steps out. He bent down and started digging.

"It should be here," he said, flipping dirt out of the

shallow hole. Cammie looked around. *What if someone catches us?*

He stopped digging and smiled. He pulled a small metal box out of the hole. "Damn, it's still here. I can't believe it." He piled the dirt back in the hole and stomped it down with his shoe. They went back to the Corvette with the metal box. Simon took a rag out of the glove box to wipe off the dirt. He shook the rag out and tossed it under the seat with the shovel. He opened the box and pulled out a plastic toy lion.

"I told myself that I'd be brave like this lion someday and when I was brave enough, I would come back to claim him." He handed Cammie the lion.

She smiled. "You are the bravest man I know, Simon Fisher."

He wiped his hands on his jeans and continued, "My mother decided we were going to call ourselves gypsies. With the little money she got from the house, she bought a caravan."

She shook her head in disbelief. "Why?"

"We traveled all over Canada thieving for a living. Stealing crap to get by. She also read fortunes. It was all a crock of shit." Simon's eyes went dark.

She could see why he hadn't been anxious to tell her about his parents. She took his hand. "Did she make *you* steal?"

He smirked. "She said I had to earn my keep. I didn't like it at first, but then by the time I was ten, I was really good at it. This went on until I turned sixteen. I got fed up. I decided that if I was going to be a thief, I could do better than the petty crap we stole. I left my sorry excuse for a mother and taught myself how to be a real thief. I knew if I could get enough money I could have the life I always dreamed about." He started the car. He turned the car and left his childhood home behind him. "I haven't seen Scott since I was eight and Lucy since I was sixteen. We all went our separate ways."

Her heart ached for him. *No wonder he didn't feel like sharing his past with me.* "Do you want to try to find either of them?"

"No."

"I'm sorry. That's horrible. You must think I'm a spoiled brat after complaining about my childhood."

"I did think you were once, until I really got to know you. After all, you did have the parents that I could only dream about."

A tear slid down Cammie's cheek.

He looked at her. "Hey, none of that. I turned out okay, right?"

She wiped the tear away. "Yes, you did."

"There's a happy ending to my sad story. I have two more places to show you."

*****

They walked up the steps to a Canadian Bank. Simon had explained it was one of the largest in Canada. He opened the door for her. It smelled like money as soon as they walked in. *Why is he bringing me here?* A long line of customers stood before them. They waited with the other customers for about five minutes. Simon pulled her close and put his arm around her.

He whispered in her ear, "Do you see all the security they have here?"

She looked around without moving her head. There were armed guards and cameras everywhere. She nodded, nervous. *What is he planning on doing?*

He let go of her and said loud enough for anyone to hear, "I forgot my wallet." He smiled at the customers as he took Cammie's hand and pulled her out of the line. They went back out to the car. He laughed at the confused look on her face. "I wanted to show you how secure that bank is."

She looked at him, still confused.

"When I was twenty-three, this is where I met your father. I was about to do something really stupid and he stopped me."

Cammie's eyes widened. "What were you going to do, try to rob it?"

"Yes. I got greedy. Your father could spot a thief and he spotted me. Just as I was about to make my move, he pulled the-I-forgot-my-wallet-act and dragged me out like I just did to you. I was so surprised. I didn't know what to do except to follow him out."

Cammie's eyebrows rose. "What was my father doing there?"

"Nothing illegal. He has an account there."

"Oh. Okay." *Thank goodness.*

"He took me under his wing. Later, I found out that was probably because of you. He missed you so much. He treated me like his son."

She smiled with tears in her eyes. "Wow."

"So see, I turned out okay and that was because of Max. If I would have gone through with my insane plan and tried to rob the bank that day, I would have gotten caught and probably shot."

"I'm glad my father saved you." She kissed him.

"Me too. I want to show you where your father took me." He started the Corvette and drove.

About thirty minutes later, they were sitting in front of an art museum. Cammie looked over at Simon, confused. "He brought you to an art museum?"

Simon nodded. "Let's go in."

They walked into the huge museum. Paintings were hung in sections. He led her to a section in the back. There weren't any paintings. Instead, there were cases filled with exquisite pieces of jewelry. Each made by a different artist. He walked her back to the largest case. He nodded to the necklace on display. "Look familiar?"

Cammie's eyes widened and she looked closer. *The same white gold necklace made of round cut diamonds with a gold medallion.* "Which one is fake? This one or the one in your room?" she whispered.

"Are you sure you want to know?" he asked.

"Let me guess, you and my father stole the real one and replaced it with a fake?"

Simon rubbed his chin. "The one you are looking at is real. The one in my room is the fake. Your father trained me to be the best thief I could be, with that necklace. I kept the replica for sentimental reasons."

"Explain, please."

"After practicing for months, we stole the real one and replaced it with a replica. No one even noticed. A week later, we switched them back. All just to prove we could do it. Your father kept me busy and kept me out of trouble. There, now you know my past."

Cammie hugged him and let her head rest on his chest. "Thank you for sharing that part of you with me."

"Was it as bad as you imagined?" Simon asked, on the way back out.

"I'm glad you are who you are." She smiled. "Now let's go home."

*****

Simon knew what he had to do when they got back. It had been a long time coming and now it was time. He had a plan that just might work. His life was about to change and he couldn't control the outcome. He took Cammie's hand and squeezed it as he drove along the curvy road. *She has to know how I really feel.*

*****

When they arrived back home, they found that Cammie's father had jetted Nora off to some undisclosed location for the weekend. They had the whole estate to themselves. Once they'd eaten dinner, Simon told her he had an errand to run and he'd be right back. She watched him leave and missed him instantly.

I can't wait any longer. The time has come to tell him how I feel. Excited, she ran upstairs to change into a sundress forgoing any panties, then ran back downstairs and left him a note to meet her at the pond. After she grabbed a big blanket and candles, she headed toward the dock. Feeling giddy, she spread the blanket out on the wooden planks and lit candles. The moonlight reflected on the still water. She looked up to the moon. *I'm sorry for what you are about to witness.*

Simon showed up twenty minutes later, holding a small, glittery gift bag. He sat down beside her and placed the little bag in her lap.

"For you."

She smiled and removed the tissue paper. A multi-colored, diamond bracelet was tucked inside. She pulled the bracelet out of the bag and gasped at the dazzle it reflected in the candlelight. The red diamond they had stolen together was set in the center of many smaller, colored diamonds. It was the most beautiful and sparkly piece of jewelry she had ever seen. *Even more beautiful than the Royce Ruby.*

She smiled as she held it up in the moonlight. "It's stunning."

Simon unclasped the bracelet and put it on her wrist. "These shouldn't stay hidden away. You're the perfect way to display them."

"Thank you." She kissed him and her heart soared. The sparkle caught her eye and she looked down at the dazzling, colored diamonds wrapped around her wrist. "That was some heist, huh?"

"Cammie Adams, you've pulled off the biggest heist of all. You've stolen something that was always only meant to be yours...my heart." He placed her hand over his chest. "I love you."

She hugged him as tight as she could and pressed her lips to his again and again, then smiled. "And I love you."

THE END

Made in the USA
Charleston, SC
23 September 2013